BULLY HUNTING

SUPRA

authorHOUSE®

AuthorHouse™
1663 Liberty Drive
Bloomington, IN 47403
www.authorhouse.com
Phone: 833-262-8899

Published by AuthorHouse 10/17/2022

ISBN: 978-1-6655-7334-4 (sc)
ISBN: 978-1-6655-7333-7 (e)

Library of Congress Control Number: 2022918969

Print information available on the last page.

Any people depicted in stock imagery provided by Getty Images are models, and such images are being used for illustrative purposes only.
Certain stock imagery © Getty Images.

This book is printed on acid-free paper.

CONTENTS

THE FALL OF PENNY

Day 1

My name is Penny. I am just over sixty years old. My husband has recently retired, and I have always been a stay home mother. Life has been busy all these years with my husband's work, my two boys, friends and relations and hundreds of other matters. Like most ordinary people, we could not realize how so many hard-fought years have passed like a blink of an eye. A couple years ago, when my youngest son moved out of home following his brother's footsteps, I had a new enemy to grapple with. The void. Rooms were so empty that they echoed to me. Sometimes I shut my ears and closed my eyes. When I woke up at night, I felt someone was sleeping in those rooms. They were never meant to be empty.

I was waiting for the day when my husband would

retire. We had some dreams, like any ordinary couple, starting from as big as visiting exotic places like Morocco to as small as waking up late in winter mornings with a warm cup of tea. There was another thing that always attracted me. That was to count waves sitting on a beach. I loved water, beaches, warmth, and sunshine. To my surprise, my husband had also planned something similar. One day, he announced that we should move to a small house by the shore, for just the two of us. No more void, no more fear of hearing strange voices around the home, no more traffic, crowd and pollution.

The new house had everything. A two minutes' walk from the beach, a small garden at the backyard, a lovely neighborhood; everything that I had wanted. I started to decorate my newly found abode with ample time and attention. Besides the home, there was plenty of relaxation. Every morning, we would visit the beach; take a long walk by the shore, breathe the freshness and count the seagulls and tiny boats far away. The day would go on cooking, reading, napping, watching Netflix, drinking and occasionally, talking to our children. Life turned out to be a bed of roses. I was happy, and content.

But then, someone told us that there was a virus that was going to kill millions of people. Like everyone else, we were locked in. A month passed. Another passed.

Then another. We spent time watching television and drinking and more drinking. Our initial romantic phase of the newly found happiness was fading. We needed a change again. Perhaps a holiday. A holiday from the eternal holiday. However silly that might sound.

Today, after a year since the virus attacked our country, we have stepped out of our neighborhood. It's not just out of the neighborhood but a drive of more than one hundred miles to a holiday location that has numerous memories from our past. It was the best decision to select a place like that. I could not think of anything better. My children loved to come here. We would rent the same house every time, run the same chores, visit the same attractions around, but every time we did that, my children loved it more and more.

We checked into the same home again. Over the years, the owner continued renovating the home. Some of its parts now don't match to where my children had earlier visited. Still, it soaked me into nostalgia. I could feel my boys running around the home. They could catch the spiders on their palms. They would show me, "Mum, look, skinny legs". They would let the spider go eventually but still, continue looking for more. Sometimes, they would throw stones at the birds in the backyard, or simply run at the open field behind.

Sitting in my bedroom that had a large window

facing the backyard, I was recollecting the fun filled days from the past. Why was I being so emotional? I don't know. Ever since I stepped in here, my heart feels weak. It could be the long gap of being normal after the pandemic. Or could be something else, related to my age.

My husband has opened a bottle of single malt. He offered me a glass. I don't mind. At least it will relax my mind.

Day 2

We decided to visit the center of the town like we always had done. There was quite a modest size of crowd looking for some entertainment there. People had been exhausted sitting at home for over a year. They were waiting for some fun, even if it was a small place like this. Everyone still wore masks, well, at least most people did; removing only when they were eating or drinking. The place looked like an annual conference of bank robbers. We walked around together. My husband mixed some vodka in his bottle of coca cola for us to sip from occasionally when we are in the thick crowd. There was a gentle breeze and bright sun shining up ahead. After a few minutes of walking my husband felt his legs were not cooperating anymore. He sat on a bench under a tree. I told him I would visit the tea shop across the street to see if we can get a scone or something to eat. The coca cola stayed with him.

As I walked into the shop, I was attracted by its character. It was filled with sketches, all around the walls. While looking around, I was wondering if this was a new shop. I could not remember visiting it before. After picking up the scones, I was standing in the line when a man coughed from behind. These days one could not trust the sound of a cough anymore. When I turned back, I saw a man of my own height, with black hair and black eyes, staring at me. There was no way to see his face as he wore a black mask.

"Excuse me", I said, "Can I help you with something?"

He whispered, in a voice that sounded like wind blowing through two adjacent pieces of woods, "Roy has sent me here. There is a very important message for you. Meet me at the back side of the shop. Come alone"

He walked away so quickly that I could not even ask any question. I was helpless to my anxiety. Ah, I forgot to mention. It's my biggest enemy. Anxiety. Hypertension. My doctor has told me all along my life that my anxiety could one day kill me, but I had no ways to control it. There was a time I was using prescribed medication but when I googled about many personal experiences, they scared me to death, before even I was dead. I switched to natural therapies like mediation, food habits but I failed to maintain a routine. As a result, after a while I decided to find solace in alcohol. With my age, many other problems like knee pain and short sightedness started to surface but anxiety remained my most ferocious foe. My anxiety was dictating to me that I must meet the man, behind the shop. Could I have just ignored it? Or tell my husband? I could have, but my mind would never let me do that. I needed to see everything till the end, no matter how irrelevant the matter was. I needed to see what this man had for me, even if it was a prank or something dangerous.

Very soon I was walking by the lane next to the shop, occasionally glancing at the bench where my husband was sitting with the coca cola bottle. He was still absorbed in his own inebriated state. As I reached the end of the lane I turned left and there, I noticed the man standing. He appeared to be in a real hurry. His legs were shaking in a rhythm. Some people do that when they are nervous or engrossed in something very important.

I stopped near him, waved my hand and said, "You said Roy, didn't you? You mean my brother Roy?"

He uttered the words, behind his mask, in a muffled voice, "Do you know any other Roy?"

I was taken aback by his rudeness. Ignoring, I asked, "What do you want to tell me"

He looked around cautiously and then said, "Roy is sending some evidence for you. Tonight. You need to come out of your house…at night…exactly at two o'clock. I'll be waiting across the road. You will receive the packet of evidence from me"

I could not understand anything, "What evidence? What are you talking about? Why is Roy sending here?"

"I'm doing exactly what I was told. He couldn't come himself because he is out of the country… at the moment. Don't try to call him. Apparently, cops are tracking him. But he could not wait to give you the packet. It will have some pictures of your husband and his lover. They will be useful for you. He told me to mention this. Remember, two o'clock. Across the street. Come alone. Don't do anything clever. Roy will contact you soon"

The man turned back and briskly crossed the road. I was speechless. My knees were weak. Heart was thumping. I was probably losing vision as I saw the man disappearing within a moment. Where did he go?

On the way back home, I continued ruminating on our conversation. My husband had an affair! It was a shock to me. I looked at him, again and again. We have been together for over thirty years. Why did I have to hear it now? Why is Roy trying to bother me? Is it because I was not his best sister in the past? Was it some kind of revenge on my husband? Who could he have an affair with? Anyone from work? Old neighborhood? A friend's wife?

A thousand questions continued pounding my head. As the day passed, I turned weaker. I decided to stay in the room resting on my bed, drinking more and more single malt. My husband had bought many bottles of them. He joined me with pleasure. We turned on the television so that we could avoid talking to each other. Staring at the screen, I continued thinking about the situations when he had a chance to be with another woman. Many of them came to my mind, they were futile years ago as I was busy with my family and chores. But now, when I look back, I can see many possibilities. But why is Roy sending it now? Is it a fresh incident? What if I ignore it? I could not place myself in any better position after a sudden separation. What would I be doing? Living my rest of the life with his alimony? Why am I even going to see what Roy has for me? I could simply text Roy telling him to deliver whatever he has, back to my home. Wouldn't I? Then I'd have to find a specific time where my husband is not at home. These days, he's always with me. Then how is he having the affair?

We ordered room service. Without talking to each other since the afternoon, we had managed to spend the entire day; almost. The next thing is to go to bed, and then wake up at two o'clock. That ought to be the alarm in my phone, in vibration, so that I don't wake him up.

When the alarm vibrated, I sprang on the bed. I pressed the cancel button while sitting on the bed. It took me minutes to settle my mind as the sleep was already deep. I remembered what the alarm was for. My head was hurting, and my body was weak. It was the effect of continuous drinking. I am going to get dehydrated soon. I must come back quickly for a longer sleep. Turning my head, I observed my husband sleeping sideways and making heavy snoring sounds. He is not going to wake up even if the house was bombed. I tiptoed out of the room. While walking towards the main door, I bumped myself at the corner of the dining table and chair where my cardigan was resting. I felt fortunate to find it because the weather outside might not be warm at this hour. Wrapping the cardigan around me, I tiptoed to the main door. Without making a single noise, I put on the slippers, stepped out and closed the door from behind. My heartbeat was racing, and anxiety was at the peak already. Once I was out on the road, I realized that I was unable to see clearly what was in front of me.

My glasses!

I have forgotten them in the bedroom. I could see only patches of darkness in front of me and all around. Perhaps there was no streetlight here. I could not remember how it used to be before. I convinced myself, it's not a coincidence but local authorities are indeed running short of money to keep the lights on at night. My phone light could work as a torch. As my hand reached inside my pocket, I realized that I had forgotten my phone too. A sense of fear was trying to embrace me. Was it a good decision at all? I could still just return to the house and get back to bed. I didn't need to know Roy and his investigation. But again, my desire to know something till the end started controlling my mind.

Thinking twice, I stepped forward. One step, two steps, towards the other side of the road, where I could see a contour, something like a lamppost or a tree or could be a man. I could not tell for sure. It was ghastly and unnerving. Another step, and right then I felt like I was pushed from the side, so hard that my body went up in the air; my ears were blocked with the air pressure, the right side of the body went numb, and my heartbeat went out of control. As I floated in the air, I thought of my children; their faces, for a fraction of a second. At that moment, I realized that I was going to die.

Holding the steering wheel with his right hand, James was trying to scratch his shoulder with his other hand. He was visibly uncomfortable. Tiara was hoping that his distraction lasted long so that she could avoid any conversation. While James continued his adjustment, Tiara pulled down her side of the glass slightly, enough to let some fresh air in. Winter morning air was cold and dry. Tiara, still breathed in and then closed the glass gradually.

This morning started abruptly and very differently from her routine. On her regular winter mornings, the alarm in her phone would be snoozed for two or three times before she could move out of the comfort of her bed. Her mother, Barbara, if home in the morning, would still be in bed wrapped in a duvet, while Tiara, stepping into her running tracks and sneakers, wearing a light jacket, would lock the door from outside and run at a slow pace first turning right in her alley, which would still be under the cover of early morning's last spell of snug before the sun came out. Exactly after crossing four houses, the alley would merge into a wide enough lane to hold appropriate pedestrian sidewalks which eventually would merge into a two-lane road with larger lanes for bikes and joggers. Tiara would meet and greet some of the fellow early risers, pass by the park which would still lay empty, run until the intersection to high street before turning back. Returning to her alley would complete more than three kilometers and demand Tiara to remove the jacket as her body temperature would rise, along with the sun from the corner of the alley. Tiara would glance at the fresh crimson sun if any pieces of nomad clouds were not covering it. Standing at her door she would enjoy the mystic layer of darkness being benevolently removed from her alley, as if a blanket was removed to wake up everyone in the neighborhood. Moments like that were rare as frequent drizzles, sometimes heavy rains, would almost always accompany her mornings all around the year, all seasons; often shortening her run or completely canceling it. Still, Tiara would eagerly wait for those moments of the winter mornings. Summer, less so. Summer mornings would already be bright enough to remind her that her surroundings in the alley were not pretty. Homes of people with income towards the lower side, would display their faded paints, broken chimneys, windows waiting to be repaired and rugged front yards. On the street of her main running track, early morning driving lessons would pile up tens of cars in a row, some of them honking occasionally creating unpleasant noise all around. On her return, Barbara would be up in the kitchen preparing some coffee for both of them. When Barbara was on night duties, Tiara would prepare her own breakfast, have a shower and browse her phone for news and social apps until Barbara returned, exhausted and exasperated with her life.

Tiara looked at James. He was focusing more on driving now. James was a big man with a gray beard. His voice was loud, many decibels higher than Tiara's. It matched his personality really well. He was experienced in working in multiple cases already. Tiara had met him during the training sessions and realized that he could turn out to be a potential problem for her. A problem that had not been cured even after changing five jobs until now. A problem that had been chasing Tiara for many years, right after her days of childhood. A problem of being fragile, diffident and awkward in front of someone who was physically and emotionally much stronger than her. Barbara believed Tiara was creating excuses because she was lazy and comfortable staying home. The day Tiara left her third job Barbara had a long conversation at the dinner table, suggesting Tiara should go to therapies without any delay. Tiara tried assuring Barbara that it was only a matter of time she would be in the right place around the right set of people. Then she would turn into a woman full of confidence and assurance. Barbara reminded her that the girls around Tiara's age had already been settled in jobs or family lives all around. She was perhaps the only one remaining. Tiara argued that not many had a childhood like her. Barbara wanted to move on, from all memories of the past, Tiara's childhood and even before. Tiara would continue holding on to them, waiting for a magical cure of her current situation as well as the disturbed past.

James turned to Tiara and asked, "Do you know what's the best part of a morning?"

Tiara shook her head realizing it was time James would start talking. Tiara observed that from the day she had met James. He was one of those people who loved to advise everyone, especially the ones that looked vulnerable. His advice ranged from work ethics to principles of living a successful life. When he spoke, his loud voice captured the air with a natural command which was hard to be ignored. He meant authority. And that was exactly why Tiara realized that he could be a problem for her, if assigned to the same case,

James continued, "It's our mind. Our minds are fresh in the morning. We think faster. Before we arrive at the scene, we can prepare ourselves, about all possible questions that we are going to ask. It's important to ask questions to yourself, especially when you are new" - he glanced at the road and continued, "When you are new, you are unaware of the drill of real situations. We learn a lot in training, follow all instructions and theories but this is for real. You need to be prepared to bring the best in you"

"You are a wise man, James" - Tiara looked at her phone again, to avoid further conversation. Road in front was empty. Tiara could see as far as the headlight could show her. Sun was going to be rising any moment now.

"Do you ask yourself questions?" James wasn't in a mood to give up. Tiara turned back to him.

"What kind of questions, James?"

"Like you know, are you prepared for your first case? What are the steps you need to follow during the investigation? How are you going to interrogate the people at the scene? "

"We have been training. Haven't we? I am just going to follow what I was taught. Or do you have something else in mind?"

James raised his left hand, smiled partially, "I know I know. Like I just said, training is not real life. Today is like your exam day. I'm not suggesting how you handle it though. This is your case young lady. You'll be leading it from the front. I'm just going to be there to help you if you need anything. Listen, I've done this multiple times. I know how these things usually go. You'll be surprised that most of the time they are all similar. And it's always the man, who gets into trouble in the end"

To avoid conversation, Tiara quickly browsed a routine check in her Snapchat and Instagram. She knew that James was not going to stop. When Tiara mentioned to Barbara about James she had shrugged with disappointment, "There you go again. Stop making excuses. You need to grow up. Besides, this is not even a job. I don't know why you are even doing this".

Tiara had replied, "It's for experience mum, to build my confidence"

"Your confidence will be crushed. I hope you know that. In the army and police, officers speak to subordinates in the toughest possible manner. Do you think you'll be able to handle that? You could not even take in the harmless manager yelling at you"

"But the manager was a bully mum. He bullied me all along. But just because my officer is a tough guy doesn't mean that he's a bully. You are comparing two different things mum"

"Whatever. A job that doesn't pay is not a job"

"I've always dreamt of joining the police. You know that"

"Everyone had hundreds of dreams in childhood. How many of them work at the end?"

"But this will help me mum. Even if I stay there for a few months, it's going to build my confidence. For a change, I'll be the person people will be careful to mess with"

"You think so? Do you know how crazy people on the streets are? They'll be yelling at the cops, keep that in mind. And there'll be this tough colleague of yours. Don't come back to me later, crying that your colleagues and even common people are bullying you"

Barbara advised Tiara to play a mind game with her own mind. Apparently, Barbara had heard from someone that the human mind is capable of building imaginary defense lines around it. All Tiara had to do was to imagine layers of circular fences or walls or sandbags used in warfront, whatever suited her at that moment, surrounding her to prevent anyone from entering her comfort zone. Her mind needed to build the layers of as many circles as possible. Tiara liked the idea and exercised it once. She could only build ten layers in her mind before she was distracted, and the concentric circles collapsed at once.

Tiara was quickly building the circles of sandbags, one, two, three…as James continued, "So, tell me Tiara, what are you going to ask at the beginning? Because this is your first case, I assume you are excited. Aren't you"

Before Tiara nodded James continued, "Every case is exciting but the first one is always special, you know what people say about the first kiss, this is a somewhat similar feeling. I remember my first one very well. And will always remember. The thing is, when you train you know the methods but…"

The sandbags were holding on well. Tiara interrupted by filling him in, "The real life is a bit different"

Slightly offended, James continued with a deeper voice, "There are good guys and bad guys and more bad guys. People are on the run…"

"James, this is just domestic violence. People are not so bad here", Tiara said interrupting James again.

"Are you saying domestic violence is not a big enough crime? You think those guys are not criminals? I have seen attempted murders in the domestic violence. I had to find the bad guy as if I was chasing a killer. You call that anything less for god's sake?"

"Forgive me I didn't mean that. You must have done a great job. But I was just saying that…I'd be much more excited if it was even a small theft. I was hoping I'd get to solve a crime where I don't know who I am looking for. This is the first case, like you said, I wanted it to be a special one. I'll have to admit that I am a bit disappointed"

Additional sandbags were added up.

The transmitter buzzed with control instructions and information, creating a vibe of urgency inside the car. Tiara had imagined herself inside a police car heading to a serious operation. This was sort of her dream come true, but she wasn't as excited as she should have been.

James was stroking his right index finger on the steering wheel in a rhythm. He was perhaps humming a tune while waiting for Tiara to continue.

Tiara lowered her eyes staring at the dashboard of the car. It was an old used car with patches of faded blue colors in corners of the vents and the entertainment system. The navigation system was working fine, and the radio for the control too. According to the navigation, they were only five minutes away from their destination. The radio continued with blurred noise. Tiara was not paying attention to it. She looked outside the window.

James broke the silence, "Just one last advice from me. When I was doing my investigations I paid attention to every little detail, even if it's as small as the husband doesn't use deodorant. When we get there, I want you to look around every detail before forming any opinion.

You'll be talking to the victim. I'll check with security system related things from in the building and will run the formality work. I'm encouraging you to take the front step because this is your chance to learn from a real incident"

Tiara realized that James was looking at him. She gently nodded her head to acknowledge. His words echoed in her mind, "I want you to…", "I want you to…" Tiara's mind traveled back to her earlier jobs. She had been in various roles; starting from a waiter to a makeshift actor. It was all along the same story for her. Someone somewhere was always waiting for her, to crush her confidence, to throttle her normal flow of growth as an individual. These memories haunted her at nights, often even in days. Tiara had no shortage of idle hours, when she was at home alone browsing the phone or watching a video streaming. A tiny reference or a familiar scene in the video could trigger her flow of memory, pulling her down towards depressing next few hours. These memories would stretch all the way back to her childhood, where it had all started, her home, her neighborhood, people around, the group of girls she wanted to be part of and the leader of the group, Stella.

James was probably speaking a lot more words, but Tiara's mind was impenetrable. She could hear his concluding sentences, "I hope that you succeed in your first investigation. When I went to my first one, I emerged as the winner. There was no looking back. We need to be the winner at every stage of life. Nobody remembers the loser. That is exactly why Waterloo station is not in Paris but in London"

Trying to ignore what James was saying, Tiara, again browsed her phone and then concentrated on the road. They were indeed very close to Waterloo station. With a sharp little turn into a narrow lane that was constructed no more than ten years ago, they arrived in front of an enormous building. Tiara could not see the top of the building by looking up from the car. She recognized it from the pictures she had seen before, as one of the tallest buildings in this part of the town. James drove the car inside the gated entrance and parked at the side of the walk area, blocking the road to the entrance partially. It was a sense of importance. They were the police. She glanced at James who was already outside stretching his arms. They walked towards the building.

Inside, an old man in a security guard uniform was looking at the monitor. He stood up with respect and his face indicated curiosity.

"We are here for Miss Scarlett Scott", James spoke with a commanding voice.

"Nineteenth floor. Nineteen O two", Said the man promptly.

"Thank you. I'll come back to you for some questions, if you don't mind", James said.

"'Absolutely sir. I'll be here all day"

They walked to the elevator.

"It was supposed to be you talking", James laughed.

Tiara wasn't prepared for that. She said obediently, "You were too quick. I didn't get the chance"

"Don't worry. You're going to learn how to grab your chance. They don't come for free", James was looking at the elevator interior which was decorated meticulously with spotless mirrors and bright lights. A heater was controlling the temperature perfectly all along the walkway and continued inside the elevator as well.

Soon it reached the nineteenth floor. When they knocked on the door, it opened after a couple of minutes. A ginger woman with long hair stood at the door. She was an inch shorter than Tiara. Her face looked dry, hair messed up and eyes red as if she had not been sleeping all night. She wore a black tee and pink shorts and red frame glasses in her eyes. Tiara could not guess her age, but she appeared to be slightly older than Tiara.

James looked at Tiara indicating she should start.

Holding her identity card in her right hand, Tiara said, "I am special constable Tiara, and this is my colleague, James. Did you make the phone call?"

2

Inside the apartment, the door opened to the hallway which forked at both sides, one to the bedrooms and the other to the living area. The slightly open closet door showed glimpses of a stunning collection of women's shoes. It was a large apartment with a large living area. Walls were covered with floor to ceiling long glass windows that overlooked the city buildings surrounded by the river. Tiara was awestruck for a moment by the magnificent view as she had never seen anything like it. Then she walked into the living area following Scarlett. There was a large coffee colored rug at the center of the area, surrounded by five casually positioned comfortable looking deep blue cushioned sofas. They looked expensive. The wall behind was painted with orange color and a light green credenza stood in front of it; holding a painting from the surrealist era, accompanied by 2 bronze sculpture pieces at both sides.

Right beside that tall bookshelf made of light wood color provided sharp contrast. The bookshelf had books and many other decoration pieces positioned carefully between the books. Tiara had seen a room like that only in fashion magazines. She admired the ambience.

Sofas had not been dusted; there were food particles, possibly dropped from potato chips consumed by people sitting on them recently. She must have had a party last night.

Tiara noticed that James was still on the other side of the apartment. She wasn't sure what James was doing. Scarlett had already positioned herself on another chair at the opposite side of the room where the dining table was located. The chair was made of red leather and there was a matching ottoman in front of it where Scarlett was stretching her legs on. Tiara noticed that the table was made of a glossy black wood as if it was polished every day. There were four chairs around it. Behind the dining table was the kitchen area.

"Tell me, miss Scott, what exactly happened?" Tiara said first, clearing her throat. A sense of excitement ran through her spine while saying a line that she had only seen in movies. At the same time, she was cautious and nervous; trying to avoid any dip in confidence by any means.

Scarlett took a deep breath and said, "You can call

me Scarlett. That would be more comfortable. I was under attack. That's why I made the phone call. You see it's here", Scarlett turned her head slightly to the right. Tiara could see a cut, not deep but almost six inches long around her neck. She walked near and bent to look at the cut. It was looking fresh, possibly a few hours old. A sharp object like a knife touched the skin at the surface and dragged away.

"Holy Christ! This is ominous. When did this happen? How did you stop the blood?", Tiara thought she would have to call for medical help.

"I have dressed it a little. Was able to stop the blood by pressing on it. Thankfully it didn't go deep...only because I was able to turn myself back to dodge his attack. It was a horrible moment", Scarlett was speaking like a machine in a gloomy voice.

Tiara noticed that James was standing by the door silently.

Tiara kneeled down in front of her. "We need to get this dressed up quickly. James will get the medical help right away", She looked at James as if she was sending an order. James took it positively and picked up his phone to call for help.

Tiara placed her right hand on Scarlett's hand and said, "Scarlett, tell me how it happened".

Scarlett was motionless. She was looking at the floor.

Tiara thought she was probably collecting thoughts. The floor was made of golden colored wood. Like everything else in the apartment, the floor looked expensive too.

"We had a party last night", Scarlett continued in her dry voice, "Some of my friends came over. After the party everyone left except Damien. Then we went to bed. Towards very late at night, he woke me up and started quarreling with me. He was so angry that he picked up the knife from the kitchen and tried to hit me. Although I could save myself, I was extremely terrified…I ran to the bedroom and locked myself in. After about ten minutes…I could hear the door sound of him leaving. I was able to stop the blood as I had first aid kits in the bedroom." Scarlett exhaled big.

Tiara stood up and walked towards the window. Still unable to overcome the mesmerizing beauty of the view outside, she looked up at the sky. It was cloudy. All signs of a sunny day, that she was anticipating while driving here, had disappeared. She thought it could start drizzling any moment. The room was not cold though. There was probably a heating inside the apartment as Tiara was feeling warm in her jacket.

"Is it always warm like this inside?", Asked Tiara still looking outside.

"We must have had the heating on. You remember it was raining heavily last night? I suppose we were cold.

Do you want me to switch it off?", Scarlett was about to stand up.

"No please. It's perfectly fine", Tiara waved her hand indicating Scarlett to sit down, "During summer days, this will be a greenhouse" Tiara smiled.

"It has an air-con too", Scarlett smiled; for the first time. Tiara noticed that Scarlett had a long nose that fitted well just below the red frame glasses.

"I want you to write down the name, address and phone number of Damien in this paper", Tiara handed over her notebook and pen.

While Scarlett was writing Tiara walked towards the kitchen. It had a very minimal setup for cooking. Only a handful of pans hanging, a couple of gloves, a baking tray, unwashed since last night's cooking was lying on top of the counter, and a bunch of white paper plates were thrown beside the sink. There were wine glasses in the sink, paper glasses and beer bottles on the floor. At the corner of the kitchen, a trash can appeared to be full. Just outside that a large size pizza box was lying half open.

"I'm so sorry the house is in a mess. There was no time to clean up", Scarlett said apologetically.

Scarlett handed off the paper. Tiara glanced at it quickly.

"Damien Anderson…", Tiara said, "How old is he?"

"He is in mid-thirties"

"I assume he is not going to pick up any call at this point from any number and also will not be at home. Is he your boyfriend?", Tiara asked swiftly.

"Is he my boyfriend?" Scarlett chuckled "Yes. We have been together since the last few months. Maybe five or six", Scarlett appeared to be struggling to believe that her boyfriend tried to hurt her.

"Then why was he living in a different house?" Tiara appreciated her own thinking. She thought she was doing well, asking the right questions. She looked around. James was not there.

"We thought we could try at a slow pace before committing to move in. I wasn't sure I could actually live with him. I wanted to try out for some days…and nights. If I felt comfortable, then… you know, now I feel I did the right thing. He could have killed me any day. I'm so glad that he wasn't living here. He had such a short temper; I can't explain it to you. Sometimes, I was afraid of him…felt like he was bullying me", Scarlett sniffed a little. Perhaps she was going to burst into tears soon.

"Tell me more about him. What does he do? When will he come home?", Tiara asked, ignoring the possible outburst of emotion from Scarlett.

"Erm…He is not employed at this point of time. He tried a couple of businesses in the past but couldn't make much of any of them. I think you can catch him in the evening because he doesn't really have much to do. I suppose he's going to run away the whole day…then, towards late evening, will have all options exhausted. If you raid him in the evening he should be there"

"How can you be so sure?", Tiara asked.

Scarlett was trying to relax back on the chair. She tried to rest her head back and contracted her face muscles with pain from the wound. Then she sat straight and said,

"I just know. He has no place to go to"

Tiara strolled towards the bookshelf. Long ago, someone told her that the best way to know a person's character is to scan the bookshelf in the home. She never had a chance to try the method so far. This bookshelf had some picture frames in between the books where Scarlett was seen with a man who appeared to be her father. There were plenty of books arranged in haphazard order. Most of them were paperback novels, some about history and politics and some travelogs. Scarlett must have been a busy reader. It was not clear to Tiara how one could understand Scarlett's reading habit let alone her character.

"I need a picture of Damien. Do you have one?", Tiara said, after finishing her bookshelf examination.

"Sure, I do. Let me message you. What's your phone number?", Scarlett said promptly.

When the picture arrived Tiara's phone beeped. Taking the phone out of pocket Tiara opened the picture on screen. Damien had light brown hair and a long face. He was clean shaven in the picture. Tiara thought he was aged little above thirty.

"He doesn't look like someone who can get to this extreme?", Tiara smiled.

Scarlett's expression showed annoyance, "I don't know what you mean by that. Is there anything else you want from me before you start your search?"

"Yes. The last thing. Could you show me the knife please?"

Scarlett stood up without saying a word. Following her to the kitchen Tiara saw the large kitchen knife at the left side of the sink. It was clean and shining. Examining it, Tiara murmured, "Looks like he cleaned the knife carefully. There will be no fingerprint on it"

"Why do you need a fingerprint?" Scarlett was not trying to hide her exhaustion with the whole situation.

"I understand your frustration but please try to understand. Before arresting a man on a charge like this we need to prepare a case. We need evidence that he really has done this. All we know so far, there's a large wound on your arm and Damien left your place. Can we build a case that he attacked you?"

Scarlett scowled, "I don't believe this", She started

shaking her head, "I don't believe you could say this. Tell me…did you just change your mind after looking at his picture? Did you? Have you…already started liking him?", her last few words came from the top of her voice.

That was the moment Tiara had been afraid of. She hadn't built the circles of sandbags against Scarlett. She needed to converse, not ignore. The attack was sudden and direct. Barbara was right. Even a common person can shatter her confidence even though she appeared to be the police. She was losing as a cop. Barbara one, Tiara nil.

Gathering some strength in her voice Tiara replied, "You can't talk to police like that…"

"I sure can. You're not a real police officer…you… you're a special constable," Scarlett used her fingers to indicate quotes around the word special, "I know exactly what that means. You're an amateur, aren't you? You don't permanently work in the Met but you're just a volunteer…and the most important thing…you…don't get paid for what you do. Does anyone care what you are doing? I don't think so. Does anyone care about my situation? My boyfriend tried to kill me, for god's sake. And look who they sent for investigation? Remarkable sense of responsibilities" As Scarlett walked angrily towards the hallway, James was standing there with a straight face. There was a young man beside him. Tiara shivered thinking how pleased James must have been watching her failure.

"The medic is here", said James politely.

"I don't need one. I can manage without you.", Scarlett was still fuming. She pushed her glasses back towards the head as they were trying to loosen up. Then she sat on the chair again. Tiara slowly walked around without looking at Scarlett.

"Look, Miss…", James was interrupted by Scarlett promptly.

"Call me Scarlett"

"Yes. Of course. Scarlett. You must have medical attention right now. It could get serious soon".

"Right then", Scarlett exhaled, "I'm all yours", She raised her gaze at the young man. He jumped into action without wasting a second and within a few minutes was able to clean and wrap around a bandage. He also injected something into her right arm. Tiara thought it could be for tetanus prevention or could be to avoid any infection.

"There's nothing to worry about. I'll send a prescription to your GP right away. You should be fine very soon", The man said while writing something down in a notebook.

"I'm fine. Already. I'm in great hands", Scarlett uttered with expanding nostrils. She was upset.

After the man moved out of the apartment, James looked at Tiara and said in his heavy voice, "I checked the surveillance camera recording. I couldn't see anyone leaving the building too late in the night. Maybe I missed the timing. When was it again? I was checking between three to four"

Scarlett was starting to calm down, "I think it was later than that. When did I call you?"

"Around six", Tiara said thoughtfully.

"So it must be right before that"

"Fine. I'll check around that time", James turned around towards the door.

"You see what I was just saying. You still don't trust me. You are trying to find evidence of Damien leaving the place. Are you serious?", Scarlett was starting to get sarcastic.

"Look Scarlett, it's just a procedure. We trust you and believe everything that you've said so far. Just tell me one more thing, if you please", Tiara was looking into Scarlett's eye this time. Only for a moment, they appeared torn, deep from inside. Tiara had seen such an expression before. But they disappeared as Scarlet dropped her eyes down.

"What do you want to know?"

"You keep saying…your boyfriend…Damien tried to kill you? Why do you think so? What must be his motive to kill his girlfriend?"

"It wasn't on purpose I suppose. He was just angry, out of control. He goes bonkers very easily"

"Is he always aggressive like that or last night…was anything different?"

Scarlett was quiet for a moment. Tiara thought she wouldn't answer. Scarlett stood up and walked towards the window. Sky had turned darker, and drizzling was intensifying, making the city and the river appear hazy.

"It was different than usual. He wanted money… right away" Scarlett whispered.

"Why does he want money?"

"He is bankrupt. He has no money. He couldn't work out anything. There was some business before where he made nothing. I gave him money to publish his book. It flopped. No one read it. Even when we pushed the book to the people we knew, no one praised him. He lost all hopes. He asked for money to publish another book. One day he said he was starting a new business and needed money. Last night he asked again. I lost my cool completely. I told him we would talk in the morning. He woke me up early in the morning and insisted on the money. He said he was writing a new book", Scarlet paused for breathing. Tiara had noticed that Scarlett needed exhaling quite often. She could have been on some sort of medication already.

"He's a writer... interesting", Tiara exclaimed.

"Let me show you...", Before Tiara could say anything, Scarlett walked towards the bookshelf with a lot of excitement. She pulled a book out with a smile on her face.

"Here it is", She passed the book towards Tiara. The name of the book was 'Omni- a way of life'. It had a sky-blue hard cover with white shades in between simulating white clouds on a blue sky.

"Is this a religious book?", Asked Tiara.

"That's exactly what the problem is. People think it is one and that's why no one wants to read it. There are plenty of religious methodology books like this in the market. I think his mistake was not being careful about the name and the cover. I wish he had little more guidance from the publisher"

Tiara turned the back side of the cover where author's description was available

> *Author Damien Anderson attempts to explore one the oldest evils in the human mind and seeks a remedy to prevent it. This is his first book. Damien grew up in north London. An avid reader, he also loves skiing and fishing.*

"Look, Scarlett, I appreciate your enthusiasm but I'm not really in a position to read this. I'm not a reader kind. I could try if this has an audio version", Tiara spoke with an apologetic manner.

"I know. Some people have asked for the audio and online versions, but they are not developed yet. This will help you understand Damien better, you know. He is crazy...completely...but got some valid points", Scarlett was still encouraging, "Can you please keep it with you...please... you don't have to read it now. There's no rush. Really. Read it when you get some time"

"But... I can't buy it from you... I am not supposed...", Before Tiara finished, Scarlett held her hands tight, "You're just borrowing. Not buying. Don't worry", She smiled.

"Okay okay... I'll keep it. But again, my job is not to understand him but to catch him, so you know"

"Of course. You just need to find him first"

Tiara looked at the watch. She didn't realize how a couple of hours had already passed. The room was still very warm despite dark clouds and rain outside. There were minor thunders as well. It was going to be a long and wet day.

"I'm going to leave shortly but before that just a couple of more questions. I know you have not eaten anything since morning, and you also need rest. I'm going to be very quick now"

"Of course", Scarlett smiled again.

Tiara smiled back, "What do you do Scarlett? I mean as a profession."

"I work for a realtor, assist in finding rental properties"

"And you own this…entire thing?" Tiara rolled her eyes in a circle to indicate the perimeter of the apartment.

"It's a gift. From my father"

"The man in the picture?" Tiara pointed out to the picture she had seen on the bookshelf earlier.

"Right. He lives in the states, Brooklyn. He's a fund manager or something like that. He gifted this flat to me when I turned twenty. He also sends me money every month and there are finances around my name. I don't really have to do any work, but days are boring without doing anything meaningful"

"And that's how Damien knows you could fund him?"

"Yes. He knows my father will never say No if I asked any money"

"Interesting. How often does your father visit you?"

"Once a year or even less. He's quite a busy man"

"Your mother?"

"She passed away. Many years ago…", Scarlett replied mechanically without any grief in her face.

"I'm sorry. Any other relatives in London?", Tiara was noting down some of the key points in her notebook.

"Uncle and his family. He's my mother's younger brother. I lived with them for the most of my life. They are kind of like my practical parents."

Tiara had more questions rising up, but she thought probably not relevant to the case. Then she asked, "How about Damien? Is he English?"

"No. His parents migrated from South Africa when he was very young"

"Do you have his parents' address? It's possible Damien is trying to hide there."

Scarlett shook her head to the sides, "I'm afraid I don't have the address."

"Not a problem. We'll find it. I think that would be all. James will get in touch with you within an hour or so once the report is completed formally and if anything, else is needed. You have my mobile number, do call me directly if you hear anything about Damien. I'll let you know as soon as we find him"

Scarlett shook her hands with a smiling face. Tiara walked out of the door slowly. While waiting for the elevator she looked back once to find Scarlett was standing at the door. Initial bitterness of the encounter had disappeared. Scarlett wasn't so grumpy after all. Tiara had a sigh of relief and also had a sense of satisfaction. She thought she had done well. Next task was to find James.

3

James disagreed to come with Tiara for further investigation. Tiara had a hard time explaining to him why she needed to lead the search by herself. James, almost raising his voice, was questioning Tiara how she was unable to handle Scarlett much professionally. James believed that Tiara had miserably fumbled at her first investigation and should be removed from the case. After Tiara's pleading effort to convince him for one last chance, he agreed for Tiara to investigate Damien's address, phone number and other records, while he himself would continue reporting the case formally. While parting their ways, Tiara had to rely on the buses or underground trains to continue her work as James decided to take the car.

The rain, the dark sky and gloomy roads, were not enough to cast more shadows in her mind than what James's behavior was creating. Tiara walked on the pathway looking at the roads where people rushed to work ignoring the weather. Tiara was at work as well but in a strangely different way. It was supposed to be her case, but she didn't even have the car. As she continued stepping into the road soaked with rain, her footstep splashed water around. Looking at the water, she was losing concentration. Memories of her past five jobs were trying to appear like flash cards in her mind. She needed to build the barriers again; a much powerful one, like electric wires. With every job she worked on, she received a bully, as if they were gifts from the employers. This job too, was turning out to be similar to the earlier ones. Many times, she had asked Barbara whether it was the same in Barbara's career, but Barbara always carried a different view of the world. She had never believed that anyone could be nice to her anyways. Tiara had been disagreeing with such a grim outlook, but her patience was running out. Maybe, Barbara was right again.

Before entering the tube station Tiara made a phone call to Glen at the headquarters. It felt so real; almost like a field agent calling the headquarters in an action movie. At last, she was up to something useful.

"I am looking for this man. Glen, sending you the name, number and address. See if you can pull up something", Tiara instructed over the phone.

"Let's be real Tiara. I've got too much at this point. I can't get to it at least in next three or may be five hours"

"That should be fine. If you could also pull up all other Damien Anderson's details, will be great"

"As you wish"

"Owe you a beer. I'll wait to hear from you. Oh... wait, ...one more thing", Tiara suddenly remembered.

"What now?" Tiara wasn't sure Glen was genuinely busy or pretending to be busy near her. They had met just a couple of times during his presentation to the trainees and for some unknown reason, after the session, he had approached Tiara for a coffee. During the coffee Glen had told Tiara that he was single, lived with some roommates, a workaholic, was from Wales where his parents were still living, and he was obsessed with video games. Over the coffee they had discussed science fiction movies that Glen loved the most. Tiara was never a big fan of the genre, but she too liked The Ready Player One. Glen could go on and on by extending his imagination of a future where people have virtual families and are babies being born virtually. Tiara listened to his ideas and expressed her opinion that transforming emotions into a virtual world, would leave the real humans lonely. Glen didn't think that the world was any better at the moment. Tiara had felt momentarily that Glen was speaking like her mother. Glen wanted to continue to another date, but Tiara had not responded since then. She was wishing Glen had already found someone else before making the phone call today. Wishing that again in her mind, she continued, "If you could also check in the South African embassy with that name. According to the records this man had migrated when he was a child, could be around early nineties"

"And...?"

"Just wanted to verify... that he indeed came from South Africa and if we could get to his parent's address"

"Alright. You will hear from me very soon".

While sitting in the tube, Tiara was thinking of Glen. What made him interested in Tiara? She could not think of much. She examined herself in the reflection of the tube window. The mirror in her own bathroom, every day showed her reflection whenever she was interested in paying attention to herself. Before going for the morning run when she looked at the mirror, she could see a miserable girl, trying to avoid yet another futile day. At night, before going to bed, her reflection looked defeated. Even after painting her eyes with liners at times, to remove the fatigue around her eyes, the mirror, somehow, never lied. It was a magic mirror which always reminded Tiara that she had not won any battle yet. Today, in her Met uniform, she appeared much stronger and confident. She wanted to test her expressions, by twisting eyebrows and lips, to create different moods of her police deity but the train was reasonably crowded for her not to act anything stupid and embarrass the police department. The volunteer work was something she was really looking forward to. Although her Bachelor degree would not be of any help, she was just looking to do something that could reverse the trend of her defeat in maintaining a stable job. After numerous attempts Barbara had rested her case to convince Tiara to pursue higher studies. She always insisted that the only way for people of their community to obtain upward social mobility was to focus on education. Barbara's parents had migrated from Jamaica just after the world war. Most of those islands were already part of Britain and all they needed was to board a ship that was sailing to the dreamland. The ship was called Windrush and people migrated through that were forever known as the Windrush generation. Barbara had told stories of how her parents lived in tiny apartments with ten more families in it, how they changed homes almost every month, how the horrifying infamous riot in Notting Hill had shaken their faith so much that they even were considering a return. Shortly after the riot Barbara was born, and they decided to try their luck a little more. Gradually, community homes were being built at different parts of the country where many such families started to form neighborhoods.

After years and decades of struggle, many riots and discriminations, families were finally starting to settle down in those community-based neighborhoods where their children went to schools with local children, played with them, became friends and sometimes married and had their children. These families worked in factories, shops, hospitals and many other jobs where community service was in demand. Some drove tubes and buses, some cleaned homes, some cleared litter. Few lucky ones had talented boys who played soccer and joined training camps. Girls didn't play soccer. They played with dolls when they were alone; played on the swings and slides when they were in groups. Sometimes they tried playing soccer, but men did not notice them. Many girls were destined to be nurses. Barbara had been a nurse ever since she had graduated from college. So was the woman next door in their first home. And few other women in that neighborhood.

Tiara's body was jolted by a sudden break. She tried looking around where they were. It was just one stop away from Angel where Damien's address had pointed out.

While back on the street Tiara breathed a scent of wet air that refreshed her lungs. Rain had stopped. The air was still keeping some moisture. It was a lazy Monday afternoon at this side of the city where streets are narrow, often paved with cobblestones and decorated with large graffities all around. Soon, she spotted the house. A brown brick building right at the edge of the road. The address said flat number two. The main door was ajar, but the flat door was locked. As she suspected, there would be no one at home at this point of the day. She decided to ask the neighbors, but no one was home in two other doors on the same floor as well.

Coming out of the building, Tiara noticed a Starbucks just opposite at the road. It was a good place to wait for Glen's call or a visitor in the building, whichever happened first. She also realized that she had not eaten anything since morning.

It was grilled chicken on ciabatta that filled her stomach up completely. Then she sat with a cappuccino thinking what should be done next. Her small handbag was lying on the table. She then noticed the book that Scarlett had handed over in the morning. Perhaps, it wasn't a bad idea to just browse that.

Tiara opened the book, Omni. The first few pages were filled with the author's dedication to the people who had been victim to the bullies. Quickly glancing at the chapter names Tiara noticed the first chapter is all about explaining what Omni is and then there was a series of stories. Tiara wondered what it was all about. She decided to proceed with the reading.

OMNI

I am bleeding.

When I was in my mother's womb, the safest place in the world, I was protected from everything. I was fed when I was hungry, I slept when I was sleepy. The same treatment continued after the first few weeks of my birth. I was fed many times, put to sleep many times. When I didn't like something, I cried, everyone ran towards me to see what went wrong.

As I grow up, I meet my siblings. They play with me. Sometimes the elder brother is too strong for me. He throws the ball at my face that hits my eye. I cry out loud. My mother glances at us and moves on. The cousins are stronger. They pull me off the ground and throw me up in the sky. My body trembles while I roll downwards, only hoping someone is there to catch me. I hear my cousins and siblings laughing. Sometimes, I don't have siblings. It's only the cousins laughing. I can't find my mother anywhere.

If I am from some other parts of the world, I can find

my mother struggling to prepare food for everyone else in the family. There is a lot of demand for food, everyone wants to eat. My mother can't step out of the kitchen, can't see the sun or rain or the moon most days. My father comes home drunk and beats her up into pulps. She weeps at the corner of the bedroom. Only I can find her.

If I am a boy, I watch and learn how to treat a woman. My grandmother, who lives with us, yells at my mother all the time. She is ready to find mistakes in her every second. The other family members of my father treat her like a slave. If I am in another part of the world, they torture her, abuse her, sometimes, violently and sexually. I watch in silence because I have no strength.

If I am a girl, I hide under the bed watching my mother suffer. I can't cry. I pray to god to free my mother, even if that means sacrificing my own life.

One day I start going to school. It's fun at the beginning. We play a lot, both indoor and outdoor. I make new friends. Some boys are strong. Some are fearsome. If I am a boy, they want to tear me apart. They hold my neck under their arms and push me down to the ground. I suffocate. I can't breathe.

If I am a girl, they don't look at me. Sometimes, I am oversized; sometimes, I am a wonk and sometimes, I am ugly. They shame me. The other girls who are pretty and lucky, laugh at me. If I am in another part of the world, I don't go to school. I am confined inside the four walls of my safe home waiting to get married. Meanwhile, some male relatives try me at different times. I am terrified. I can't tell anyone.

If I am neither a boy nor a girl, no one talks to me. In some parts of the world, I find my own people. They sleep in slums and beg on the road during the day. I am now one of them. At least I am not afraid anymore. If I am in another part of the world, they leave me alone. I know I have my rights, but wait, I see they are coming after me. I will be dead soon.

Moving on as a boy, I go to a college and then start looking for a job. People are racing against each other and against time. Everyone wants to finish first. My friends betray me, strangers threaten me, and my father mocks me for not being able to establish myself. I am determined and somehow find a job. If I am lucky, I am sedentary, working like a run in the mill. Nobody notices me in the beginning. But there comes someone, lurking from the corner. He steals my glory, tries to pull me down. If I am not sitting all day, I am working in a factory or a farm or on the roads or at the battlefield. I am constantly abused, by my supervisors, my commanders and my enemies. They notice that I have a different skin tone or a different religion. I don't belong to them. They ridicule me, call me by different names. My color is prominent. My religion is awkward, at my work, at the playground, at the shopping mall or war front. When I play a sport, they tackle me hard and then remind me who I am. When I am at war, I pray that I don't become a prisoner of war. I can't escape no matter where I go until I reach a place where people are of my color and religion. But guess what? Now I see, my friends are looking for someone who is different from them. It doesn't matter what they are looking for, they just want to humiliate someone, who is not like them. They want to feel the same pleasure.

If I am in an MMA ring, people come to see me. I kicked my opponent to break his teeth. People are elated. They like the blood. My opponent floored me. People continue to be elated. They are savoring my suffering. I see their faces. They are hungry for pleasure, hungry for blood. I see my cousin in the crowd, the one who had thrown me up in my childhood.

If I am a woman, when I am racing, men don't like me. In some parts of the world, misogyny is official. They hate me running alongside. In another part of the world, they manipulate me. They try to prove me wrong, at every step. Even my boss, who is another woman, dislikes me. She is insecure. I might snatch her seat one day. In another part of the world, I don't get to work. I stay home, to cook, to pretend that I am happy bearing children, as many as my family want. If my luck is worse, my husband

comes home drunk and beats me up, just like my mother.
Life has come a full circle for me.

If I am neither a man nor a woman, I am already
dead. There is no story of mine.

From the MMA ring to my own home, I am torn
apart. I bleed. Am I one of them too? When I am stronger
than someone else do I make the other side bleed?
However, that doesn't change my situation.

I am still bleeding.

I go to church, mosque, temples, synagogues to
understand what people closer to God have to say about
my sufferings. They tell me the story of Good and Evil.
God had created Evil in the minds of humans. Evil
dictates a major part of our emotions. I question why
God would do that. Why create Evil at all? Even if it was
a mistake, why not erase it immediately?

If I don't believe in God, I read about it. Try to find
the answer in science. What makes us evil? Why do we
enjoy watching others in pain? I learned a German word.
It's Schadenfreude.

I read about religions. Some of them don't think any
other religion should exist. Some show respect to other
religions but they divide their own society into many
classes. People from the lowest layer often get overrun
by the upper layers. Schadenfreude? In another religion,
every family must donate their eldest son to God. His

heart is ripped out of his chest while he is still alive. It's blood all over his body. People of God watch the blood flow.

I conclude that bloodshed is the only constant truth in human history. Hundreds of Kings invaded the globe over and over; millions of people were killed; more millions were displaced. Even until the last century, nations tried wiping out each other. People were eliminated in gas chambers, by nuclear weapons, terrorism, genocides, civil wars and riots. The Evil in our mind that God had created, is still operating and getting stronger.

I live among common people. I can't change the kings or the cardinals or the presidents or the terrorists. I want to change my life. I want to stop bleeding. I want to change the people around me, from my family to cousins to friends to colleagues. I talk to them. Tell them that the only way to destroy this Evil is to change the human brain, at birth or even before; so that the Evil part is never formed. But who can do that? And how? How many centuries of research would it take to understand the entire human brain let alone alter it?

While research continues, I need to stop bleeding, even if it's temporary. I try to explain to others. Let's not get carried away by this strange pleasure. If I make others bleed there will be my turn to bleed as well. If I go after someone, very soon someone will come after me for revenge. So why not stay in harmony? They laugh at me. They ask me, is it a new religion? I say so be it. Let's say it's a new religion but it's only about one motto, don't make anyone bleed. They say they'll think about it. I want to explain more. We, humans, are the most powerful animals. We have come a long way from the rest of the animal kingdom. We must continue our journey to a better evolution. We need to be the creature that represents everything and all being in the universe. We need to be Omni. It's only possible if we care for each other; respect the existence of others. I remind everyone to beware of the reactions of your momentary pleasure from others' misery. You are going to suffer soon. Your turn is waiting. If you believe in God, trust that God will punish you. If you don't believe in God, trust that someone else is going to punish you. Hurry up and destroy the Evil, nip it in the bud, at home, at childhood and then on. Stay united. Become Omni.

When we are Omni, If I am a man, I am also a woman. I am everything. I fear no one and no one fears me. I am myself. Just like how I was in my mother's womb.

THE REIGN OF CLIVE

Day 1

*C*live meant business. That was his first impression on me. He wore photochromic glass that turned black when he stepped out in the sun. His hair was tightly brushed behind, almost like old Italian gangsters. There were shades of beard haphazardly growing all over his cheeks. And he smoked. Almost every hour, he stepped out of the building to the designated smoking area.

I told my parents over the phone that I am looking forward to a great journey with Clive. My parents live in the far east of Yorkshire. It's called East Riding. It's so remote that most people haven't heard of the names of those places. We speak in a thick accent which makes people here glance at me twice. When I was moving to the biggest city, my parents were extremely delighted that at last both their children were going to be independent.

My elder sister has been the most brilliant student in my village. When she scored top at GCSE in the entire county, she was awarded a medal. When she was selected in the electrical engineering program at the university, my father gifted her a milky white MacBook. Her old laptop became my property since then. I rarely used it though. My mother dreamt something even bigger for me. When I was young, she claimed that I had a bigger brain than my sister. As I grew up it was clear that my sister was going to steal all moments. I was happy for her because I knew that not everyone should be doing the same thing.

When I told my parents I wanted to study history, my father went on asking everyone he knew about the prospects of someone being employed with a degree in history. He learned that the only way to make something out of history was to become a professor.

So, I started applying to universities all around. With modest school results like mine all along, it wasn't difficult to get the admission. I sat in the train to London waving my hand to my parents standing outside the window. A new life was going to start for me.

I loved the university, my dormitory, and my part time assistance job. I liked Clive too. He is my advisor. The next few years' relationship between us is going to define my career. I was excited and hopeful.

Day 67

Clive has been making my life difficult. He believes I am not smart enough. Sometimes, he utters the word retard to himself while reviewing my work. I have been demotivated for the past few days.

He told me that he was fascinated with the dark history of the vicious emperor Vlad. It's not unusual to get attracted to this particular topic. Hundreds of historians have delved into the mysterious characters and larger than life stories of Vlad. Clive was trying to find a new perspective. When I first met him, he told me that he had some ideas which are still not clear to me, even after all these months. He would ask me to read about Vlad and his time and gather some key notes for review. We sit together twice a week to review my progress and he hasn't been happy. I still don't have a clue what I'm looking for.

Day 189

I spoke to my parents today and I was almost on the verge of tears. Things around me have been difficult and I feel like I must return home. Clive has been a nasty man. He ridicules me in front of fellow students, both at work and the private parties. It especially hurts when there are girls around. They started to think that I am a retard, who wants to earn a doctorate in history but is not sure what to look for in history.

I have been following Clive's instructions diligently but all I receive is more pain and more mockery. Sometimes, I think he is doing it intentionally. There might be some phony admission process to earn government funds by showing more PhD students even though they are not of any use.

To my despair, my mother doesn't agree with me. She says leaving the study will be foolish and insulting to the family. I must stay put and focus on the work. The fault must be entirely mine.

Day 478

Clive makes me iron his clothes and shine his shoes. He doesn't believe I am good for anything else. My research has gone nowhere. I don't think it has even started. Last night I was ironing his suite while he sat in the office room talking to a student. He has been accepting a couple of more students lately. I want to tell them the truth. The scam. The obscure nature of this department. Will they listen to me? I don't believe so. I already look like a loser. I haven't partied at all lately; maybe six months or so; haven't kissed anyone. I am starting to get depressed. Everyone around is doing better than me. I haven't even started.

Day 945

My mates told me that they had to carry me home last night from the pub two blocks away. They told me I have become so heavy that they lost their breath very easily. They asked me to run every morning or work out in the gym. I know I can't because I don't wake up in the morning. Clive makes me type until very late at night. He has so many documents. Sometimes, I wonder what he is up to. I typed on his computer until my fingers hurt. In addition to that I have been polishing his shoes and ironing his shirts as always. He even tips me sometimes because I am the most loyal servant of his majesty.

I have become habituated with the fact that Clive is my owner. I am his personal assistant. That's my work. I don't have a family where I can go back to. Actually, I don't want to go back. I like this life. I read somewhere; it's called Stockholm syndrome.

Day 1945

Almost six years have passed since I came here. Now I have forgotten what I came here for. I now work at the H&M store during the day. At night I work for Clive, in his home. I clean his bathroom, arrange his dishes, and pick up his takeaway orders. His girlfriend is going to have a baby with him. Her baby bum looks adorable. One night Clive had asked me to bring a special mousse that she craved to eat. I never disappointed Clive. If I did, he would threaten me to end my career. He has done that all these years. Slowly, I have started to realize that there is no career to end. I could end it myself anytime. For now, I am keeping myself available for the baby to arrive. I think he is going to ask me to take care of the baby, like a babysitter.

Day 2750

I think I am finished with Clive. He doesn't need me anymore. He said I must leave within a week's time. I don't have the degree I had wanted so much. I could go back to Yorkshire but all these years, whenever I visited my parents, I told lies about my life. It can't change all of a sudden. I have drastically reduced my frequency of visiting them over the last three years. Still, I can't take a chance. They must not know who I actually am.

Day 2850

I can't let Clive go. It's not fair. I want justice.

4

Tiara closed the book with a confused state of mind. What was it all about? A new religion? A chronicle of someone being bullied? She had never read anything like that with her limited interest in books and stories. Her curiosity was pulling her to finish the next chapter to know what had happened to Clive, but eyes would not allow that. She had never been a reader, other than occasional newspaper or magazine pages. Books have always made her fall asleep. It was much easier to listen to Podcasts if she needed to learn anything. Even some Netflix documentaries were enjoyable. To her astonishment, she realized that she had somehow finished reading two chapters of a book which was not only non-fiction but also of a strange educational kind. She examined the book again; its blue cover could have been attractive at a first glance, but the title somehow nullified it. At the back of the book, towards the bottom, publisher's information was provided. Damien must have paid them the full money to get the publishing contract accepted. Thinking of Scarlett, she smiled; it was Scarlett who had paid the money.

Tiara didn't keep track of time. She noticed that the Starbucks was now crowded with a bunch of young men and women who looked like university students. There were many other people in the line as well. Students were noisy, thought Tiara; they were laughing at the top of their voices, trying to decide what their choice of coffees should be. Some of them were animated, explaining stories to others. At the table beside the entrance, a family was trying to adjust their little child on the pushchair. Their time of relaxation was about to end. Looking around the room, Tiara was amused, and somewhat embarrassed, at herself that she was whirling away time, by observing a mundane afternoon crowd.

"Please ring please ring…", Tiara could not help praying to herself so that her phone rang, and she had something constructive to look forward to. She was not going to describe to her mother that her first day of investigation was sitting at a Starbucks with a sandwich and a religious book. The rectangular iPhone laid lifeless in its dark green case. Tiara loved iPhone covers that came with glittering designs but after taking up this job, she had to discard her earlier phone cover that had three large flowers engraved. Tiara also had decided to sacrifice her nail and eye decorations. She tapped her index finger on the phone, once, twice, thrice. Looking at her nail she smiled to herself. It was cleaned and trimmed.

Few minutes later, after losing all her patience, she dialed Glen.

Glen picked up after an eternity of rings, "I was just going to call you Tiara"

"What did you find?" Tiara wanted to show that she had been busy.

"Well, to be completely honest with you, not much", Glen was chewing something, which must have been a late lunch.

"The photo does not match anything in our database. There are many Damien Andersons in town. If you want to chase each of them, I can email you all the addresses. The thing is...none of them are in the Angel area. The address that you've given me, is owned by someone who currently lives in Scotland. What's worse for you is, the property is rented to two women. I have their names if you want them... just a second..."

Tiara sighed at the other end. It wasn't going to be easy to chase Damien.

"Yeh... I got 'em here... ", Glen continued, "Elizabeth Hargreaves and Nadira Hadid. I have no idea how Damien could live in that house. Your best bet will be… he is seeing one of those…", Glen grinned.

"What about the embassy? Any news?", Tiara ignored the grin.

"I did. They need some time to search. It was a long time ago. They need to search old records"

"So we have nothing?"

"Nada"

Tiara disconnected after thanking Glen. She was not completely certain what the next step should have been. Slowly, she walked out of the shop. Damien had become a fugitive. Clearly, the only way was to alert all stations for a search. Her phone rang suddenly. It was James.

"What are you up to at this point?" He asked in his demanding voice.

"Just gathering the information about him…"

Tiara was interrupted by James's voice "listen, I have news for you. I've informed the headquarter about the attempted murder and also…have circulated the alert across all stations. He will be caught very soon"

"What? Wasn't I supposed to do that?" Tiara wanted to kick James in the middle of his stomach.

"I thought I could just go ahead and do it. After all, I've been doing this longer than you and I know exactly how these people run away. It's just a matter of a few days. He's going to run out of money...then absolutely no food, no place to hide...and the lad will be out on his way back to his girlfriend. I just did you a favor by doing your job. And you are welcome. I know you are using your own..."

Tiara disconnected the phone. A shadow of defeat started looming over her mind again. This time she could not build the barrier and decided to let go. A flurry of memories started to flow. As she closed her eyes, she could see the young man at the last job yelling at her. Then the one at the prior, trying to threaten her to suppress sexual assaults, and then all of a sudden, her memory travelled back many years more, where she was standing at her door, staring at the gang of young girls playing at a swing. Barbara was whispering from behind asking her to join the girls. She looked into the eyes of the leader of those girls who turned her head from side to side with the front teeth biting the lower lip, indicating Tiara dared not step forward. Tiara stayed put thinking Barbara would help her join the group, but Barbara had locked herself inside the home. She was left alone.

Sometimes, she wondered whether another neighborhood could have shaped her childhood better. Barbara always mentioned that she could not afford any rented home as she was a single mother raising Tiara.

As Tiara grew up, she had learned that people of her community had many different neighborhoods across the town. Perhaps, being in one of them could have changed her life. Later, they had to move to another place, but Tiara had already finished school and those memories were already created to stay with her for eternity.

While walking towards the station, Tiara bumped into a broken corner of the pedestrian way. Damien's book fell on the ground upside down. The address of the publishing house was just in front of her eyes. Well, that was it; a straw to clutch at.

When she reached Covent Garden station, it was towards the end of the day. Streets were overly crowded with people flowing from all directions. It was difficult to come out of the main street and find the address which was only a couple of blocks away from the Opera House, in a lane called Ealham. The brick building was three floors tall with a finely decorated store at the bottom. The woman at the counter of the store had a quick glance at Tiara and turned her eyes down immediately. Realizing that she was still the police, Tiara walked past the main door; a black heavy piece of wood with the number written on it. She had already spoken to someone from the office about her arrival. The door was left open in anticipation. She walked up to the first floor following the instructions given by the office.

Inside the office, which was a tiny publishing house, there was a large table at the side of the wall with two computers on it. One of the terminals was occupied by a young man; perhaps the person who spoke over the phone. The table was meticulously arranged with no traces of loose paper, unlike Tiara's expectations of a typical publishing house. At the diagonally opposite side, a middle-aged man sat in front of a relatively smaller table, with a computer and multiple telephones around. There were also notebooks, a photo frame, paperweight, and a water bottle on the table, providing the corner as the head of the office status.

"I am looking for Mr. Kean", Tiara turned to the middle-aged man.

"That's me", the man smiled. Tiara noticed that his front teeth were damaged at the lower side. An accident in childhood could have created that and he never bothered to fix it anytime.

"How can I help you? We usually don't get police in here. Unless you are writing a book or any of our writers are criminals, I can't think of why I should be questioned by police", Mr. Kean was still smiling, "Why don't you have a seat." He pointed to the chair at the opposite side of his own chair. Tiara pulled the chair.

While seated she glanced at the other end. The young man was focused on his own computer.

"May I get you something? A cuppa?", Mr. Kean said in a polite way.

"That wouldn't be necessary. I'm going to wrap up very quickly"

"That's absolutely fine. I'm free this afternoon. Please go on"

Before he could say any further Tiara placed the book on the table, and asked,

"Do you recognize this book?"

Mr. Kean picked it up with his right index finger and thumb. Then he adjusted his glasses and looked at the back of it, "Oh yes. I remember this one. What a waste of time. This man didn't know how to write. When I read the manuscript, I was not convinced that I'd be able to finish reading it. Have you read it?"

"No", Tiara nodded to the side.

"Please don't. It's not worth a read. He tried to teach a thing. Or maybe…more than one thing. A lesson perhaps. You see, my house is famous for its solid stuff, you know what I mean? Like how to improve your confidence, how to succeed in the corporate world. Blokes with years of experience in every field come to me. I'd never have taken this one, for sure, unless…"

Tiara waited patiently with a squinted eye.

Mr. Kean drank a sip from his green water bottle. The color resembled Tiara's phone cover, slightly less glossy though.

"Before that, may I ask you something?", Mr. Kean looked up to Tiara's eyes.

"Please go ahead", Tiara said.

"You have not introduced yourself yet. I was just wondering…uh…", Mr. Kean wasn't able to complete.

"I'm sorry. I should have done that at the beginning," Tiara showed her identity card. Mr. Kean glanced quickly at the card and smiled, "Absolutely alright. You know, these days, we can't trust anyone. Even when in Met uniform. I apologize for asking you. It was just a formality. Can you please help me understand as well… uh, why are you asking about Damien Anderson?"

"Sir, we have evidence that he has committed a heinous crime and is currently trying to run away. We are looking for him actively", Tiara said with a straight face.

"I see. Are you sure he is on the run? I mean, he must be a normal bloke, not a criminal type. You know what I mean? He's probably sleeping at a friend's place"

"How do you know he's not a criminal sir?", Tiara quickly glanced behind to the other table. The young man was staring at her. His eyes were like a pair of stones fixed on a bracelet.

"Forgive me, I didn't mean that. He may very well be a criminal. Who knows? These days we can't trust anyone. But what I'm saying is, I have no relation with whatever crime he has done. In fact, I've never seen him in my life?"

"What do you mean?"

"He never showed up at my office. Can you believe that? It's his book, his first book. Everyone, absolutely everyone, gets excited about the first book. But he wasn't. He just wasn't there. It was his partner, I forgot her name, a lovely young lady, who worked with her to get this published. I suspect it was her money as well"

"Scarlett. That's her name"

"Right. Scarlett", Mr. Kean nodded.

"Are you saying all the paperwork was done by Scarlett?"

"She mentioned that Damien was not well those days and was confined at home…we thought it was Covid…she took the papers home and got them signed. All checks were from her account. All negotiations and discussions were with her. She was like a representative… or like an assistant of the man"

"How do you allow that? How do you publish a book without meeting the author?", Tiara looked behind again. The young man was still staring. Tiara turned her eyes away.

"Honestly, we don't care. Author's representative had all the information we needed, and it worked well. It's a different discussion why the book didn't do well. In our profession, such ups and downs are common. Some books don't do well. If it was my money, I'd worry a lot more. Thankfully, it was not"

Tiara sighed. She was talking to someone who had never seen the suspect, "Is there anything else you can tell me about him? Anything that you remember?"

Mr. Kean closed his eyes to pretend that he was trying to recollect something. Tiara waited patiently for a minute or so. Mr. Kean opened his eyes and said, "Scarlett mentioned that he was working on a play... or was it another friend of hers? I'm sorry I can't quite remember. Who exactly was it? Anyhow, the play was supposed to be something related to the struggle of some Muslim people in some country...was it Iran... or Syria...or was it Saudi? I really can't remember. She wanted to know whether I had any connection who could help stage the play. But I didn't. That's all. I don't know anything else about the man"

5

When Tiara got back to the alley in Angel, the sun had already set. Chill breeze of a long rainy winter day was bracing Tiara's body. Tiara was almost shuddering even with the jacket. A large part of the road had holes lodged with water that Tiara had to avoid while walking. Starbucks was still crowded with loud music coming out of it. A couple of more stores across the streets were illuminated, providing a guided pathway in front of Tiara. It was a soggy but mysterious atmosphere.

Damien's building door was open as before. Tiara pushed the door inside. The corridor was lit up with bright ceiling lights. The wooden floor had plenty of water marks everywhere from muddy footsteps. Residents had started returning from work. As she walked, Tiara smelled spicy cooking from one of the doors. She felt tired at her legs. It was a long first day at work. And the worst was, it was not over yet.

At the second knock of the door, it opened partially, and a woman stood in front of Tiara. She looked young, perhaps in mid-twenties or close to thirty. She was of about the same height as Tiara, had long black hair straightened up with perfection, sharp features and glasses with thin steel frames. She was wearing black tights and a pale top, whose color was not very clear to Tiara in the darkness surrounding the door. She appeared to have showered immediately before opening the door. It was Nadira, Tiara had no doubt.

"May I help you?" She asked politely.

"I am Tiara, from Met", Tiara showed her identity card. This time there was no mistake.

Nadira opened the door completely and stood aside. "Would you like to come in?"

Tiara stepped inside. "I am here for an investigation. Is this the right time to talk to you?", Tiara said while observing the room. The door opened in the living room which had a very old threadbare rug at the center with some Asian designs on it, most of which were faded due to loss of threads all over. Surrounding the rug, a sectional sofa was laid facing a flat screen television, which was standing on a home entertainment center. At the other side of the room, there was a breakfast table and three chairs made of golden woods. There was a large basket of fruits on the table holding some bananas and apples. The walls were covered with traditional English wallpapers; they too were old. It was a rented home that came fully furnished, Tiara thought, no one really took care of it.

Nadira was still waiting with an anxious face for Tiara to speak.

"There is a man named Damien Anderson", began Tiara, "He's on the run. We have come to know that this is his address. I would like to know who you are"

"I'm sorry. I don't understand?", Nadira exclaimed.

"I…am…asking, who you are miss"

"My name is Nadira. Nadira Hadid. I apologize. But what did you say about the address?", Nadira was still surprised.

"Does Damien Anderson live here?"

"I've never heard that name before", Nadira said promptly.

Tiara sighed. Her investigation could never go smoothly, "Alright. Let's do it another way. Do you own this house?"

"No mam. I'm a tenant"

"Who else lives here?"

"My roommate. Liz. She's not at home now"

"And no one else?"

"No mam. There's absolutely no one else here. I

never heard the name you just told me. Did you say Damien?"

Tiara walked around the room. It was a narrow room. A wall beside the breakfast table opened towards a very small kitchen that had just one counter with burners and lots of utensils surrounding it. There was a cutting board and knife on the counter. Nadira was planning to make dinner.

Tiara opened the picture of Damien from her phone and showed it to Nadira, "Doesn't it ring any bell?"

Nadira nodded her head both ways. Tiara noticed that the color of her top was purple, but it faded badly. It was meant for home use. It had some pictures at the center, but Tiara didn't have time to examine that.

"So, I suppose, I will have to wait for your roommate to be back. When is she coming back?"

"I don't know. She usually works later", Nadira said promptly again, "Are you saying Liz is linked to this?"

"Because you are saying you never heard about the man, what else can I infer?"

Nadira lowered her head.

"Since when do you know her?" Looking at the breakfast table, Tiara asked. One of the chairs was tightly placed as if no one had ever sat there. It was unlikely anyone else was living here recently, unless the girls were extremely clever. Sofa seats were old and crumpled at places. There were no pieces of popcorn or any food particles on them.

"A year, actually little more than a year. Ever since I came to this house"

"And you don't remember seeing this man in this home or anywhere else ever?"

"No mam. Never"

"Do you know where Liz is from?"

"She is from the north. I remember...she told me...Newcastle...or something there. We don't speak an awful lot. I leave early and she comes back late. There's barely any time during the day. On most of the weekends, I go out with friends. I don't really know what she's up to or who she hangs out with", Nadira twisted her lower lips to indicate she wasn't aware much, "I'm sorry. Would you like to sit until she comes back? Can I get you something?"

"No, that's alright. That won't be necessary", Tiara smiled. Nadira smiled back.

"If you don't mind me asking, where do you work?", Tiara said to continue the conversation. She wasn't sure how long the wait was going to be. It was a possibility that Elizabeth had run away with Damien and in that case, Tiara would be waiting for them the entire night inside this little room. She could reach out to James to send out a circular once again, but the thought of James cringed her whole body. Nadira was friendly and warm. It wasn't a bad idea to wait here.

"I work in a bank. In the City area", Nadira smiled again while adjusting her long hair that was trying to cover parts of her face. Tiara noticed that Nadira wore an expensive platinum wristband. She also had a diamond ring on her right middle finger. Her nails were trimmed and colored with dark magenta shades. Tiara envied her bank job, whatever that was.

"Do you happen to know anyone called Scarlett Scott?" Tiara asked, hoping to continue some conversation.

Nadira shook her head from left to right indicating she did not. Tiara now noticed Nadira's earrings. They contained some tiny platinum pieces hanging in the middle of a silver circle. They were pretty. The same shine was reflected from her tiny nose pin that Tiara didn't pay attention to so far. Tiara could not think of why and how a man like Damien would be linked to this woman. Nadira was certainly speaking the truth.

"Let me show you her picture. If that rings any bell", Tiara opened her phone. As part of the procedure Scarlett's picture should have been taken officially and sent to her email. She was right. The email was there with a copy of the report. Tiara opened the picture and maximized it. Then showed the screen to Nadira.

Nadira's face changed to a pensive expression for a moment, but she recovered quickly. It was evident enough for Tiara to catch, "You'll have to tell me the truth, Nadira. It's important for the case"

"Erm…Actually…I… have seen this woman. Who is she? Is she an accomplice?", Nadia appeared to be disturbed.

"No. She is the victim. Our man tried to kill her"

"Oh dear! That's terrible. Is she alright now?"

"Yeh. She is fine. She was lucky as the hit was minor. Still qualifies as attempt to murder"

"I'm so sorry for her. I've seen her before. Once or maybe twice…I don't exactly remember…with Jamal. Never spoke to her. I believe they were friends"

"Who is this…Jamal?" Tiara took out her notebook to write down the names. There were too many already.

"Jamal is… was my friend. Partner. I saw this woman talking to him at a couple of parties. There used to be a lot of people. At least ten of them. Jamal and this woman were part of the same friend circle. He never introduced me to any of them. This woman, Scarlett, always dressed well. Jamal respected her a lot"

"Where is Jamal now? Can I get his phone number?"

"Unfortunately, you won't be able to…", Nadira lowered her eyes and paused. Her lips trembled and nostrils flared. It was only for a moment before she recovered, "He passed away last year. We were together until then. After that…I had to find a new place, which is this. There were too many memories out there. Too much to cry for. I had to move on"

"I am so sorry", Tiara took a step forward and placed her right in the hands of Nadira. She lifted Nadira's hand and gave it a gentle shake.

"It's alright. I've moved on. Sometimes…I get to the breaking point", Nadira's large black eyes were turning moist.

"How did he die? I assume he was about your age?"

"He committed suicide"

"What?"

"That's right. He was in chronic depression. He was struggling to settle down. He was born in a troubled family. They were poor. His father had a long story of struggle…back in their homeland. There were bondage labor jobs…almost like slavery, in the modern form. His father lived miserably, along with many others until they escaped to migrate here. Jamal knew the history and wanted people to know about it", Nadia paused to breathe and to wipe the tears that were about to break out. Tiara waited. Then Nadia continued, "He couldn't manage to find a job. It was a vague stream at the uni. Something like international religions or cultures…I don't quite remember. No one gets a job studying that.

I don't know why he had to go for it. Or he didn't have a choice because his records were not good enough", Nadira paused to sniffle,

"He wanted to write about all the horrible things that he heard from his father. I remember he wept for days and weeks. He was very sensitive. Poor little thing. I cried for his misery. What else could I do? The world didn't know there are still so many cruel systems to oppress people conveniently. Innocent people get trapped and live in dire conditions. His idea was to stage a play depicting the details of the system. He tried very hard to get it staged. I think…Scarlett was helping him on that matter. Her group of friends…joined to help him too. But it was rejected a couple of times. He had no money. I was taking care of all bills, literally everything, from groceries to Oyster cards. His depression grew every day and eventually he couldn't take it", Nadira looked away from Tiara, towards the blank television screen, her attempt to stop the tears.

Tiara's mind was processing fast. The play, about some Muslim people.

"Do you have a copy of the play? A soft copy will just be fine. I just want to see something?"

"I think I do. Let me email it to you", That gave a quick break to Nadira to divert her attention. She asked for Tiara's email address and was able to forward the file.

"Do you have copy of the report of the suicide case or any details of the officer or station handling it? If not, don't worry I can find it."

Nadira trembled for a second, "Do you think this is related? I don't understand. He died many months ago. He had nothing to do with this man who tried to kill Scarlett"

"It's just a formality. You rest assured. It's only because this Scarlett Scott is the common link here. Nothing else"

Nadira exhaled. Must have been a hard time for her.

"Why don't you sit here, at the sofa", Tiara just realized that they were standing all the while.

Nadira walked to the sofa and sat. She sniffled big again.

"Jamal was a great man. His heart ached for his father and other people. Whenever he heard any stories of powerful people bullying the poor, and the rest of the world had no idea about it, his heart always cried"

"I'm sure he was he was a great man"

Tiara strolled around the sofa back and forth. She started thinking there was no need to wait for Elizabeth to come back. Something in her mind was telling her that Jamal was the link, not Elizabeth. Damien would probably be arrested very soon by the police and there would be no need to hunt anymore. But Damien was certainly an interesting man. His involvement with different types of people made him really special to Tiara.

At last, she made up her mind. She would first verify Jamal's story.

Standing in the tube compartment, surrounded by people returning home late evening from work on an ordinary Monday night, her city appeared stoic and dull. Only change in the past twenty-four hours was her first case. A whole bunch of new names and their activities were added to her notebook now. She would now have to find all links among the characters; just like a detective would be doing in a thriller movie. Her tired legs were telling her that the end of a long day needed a large meal, a glass of red wine and a good sleep. Looking at the passengers around, focused on their respective smartphones like zombies, Tiara longed more to go home quickly. She closed her eyes recollecting the events from the day. Loud mechanical sounds between two compartments numbed her mind. She thought she would fall asleep, standing in the compartment.

6

Tiara was driving the Ford herself. No James with her this time, and she was not as early in the morning as the previous day. The tender winter sun was trying to spread occasional warmth when it was not being interrupted by regular clouds. Roads were relatively busier. A workday had already started.

Scarlett and Nadira appeared in Tiara's dream last night. She couldn't remember the content of the dream when she woke up. Ever since she was a little girl, she was able to differentiate a dream from a nightmare. In her dreams, people appeared randomly, running random actions which, she would forget easily the very next morning. On the contrary, the nightmares stayed longer and always had similar content and the same characters, with Stella leading them.

Tiara had to report to the station for briefing and discuss the next steps. Meanwhile, Glen was in touch and James was assigned to a new case that he would perform all by himself. It was a busy morning overall. The immediate plan was to visit Scarlett. She mentioned on the phone that she would be waiting at the apartment. She wouldn't go to work; a rest was due, after the assault.

At the apartment, Scarlett opened the door with a smiling face. Her neck still showed the bandage clearly at the top of her red halter top. Her hair was tied at the back with a matching red hair clip. Tiara noticed that she brushed her face diligently. She was formally expecting the visitor today.

"Would you like some green tea?", Asked Scarlett as Tiara stepped inside.

"No thanks. I'm at work.", Tiara said with a smiling face.

Scarlett shrugged with twisted lower lip, "It's not alcohol", and smiled, "I'm on antibiotics, so no alcohol strictly"

Scarlett walked towards the kitchen and Tiara followed. From behind, Tiara noticed that Scarlett had a tiny tattoo at the corner of her right shoulder. It was visible this time as her hair was tied up. Tattoo had a thick black circular background with a red flower painted on it. Tiara could not comprehend what flower it was.

Scarlett poured the tea in a milky white cup. She was

already in the process of preparing the tea before Tiara arrived. She elegantly placed the cup on a matching saucer.

"Let's have a seat", Scarlett walked to the sofa and Tiara followed silently. After placing herself comfortably, Scarlett held the cup near her nose and inhaled with closed eyes, "I love green tea so much. It detoxifies, especially when I'm tired. Do you drink tea?"

"I do at times. Mostly, I'm a coffee girl. I have to start my day with a coffee. I can't function if I don't have coffee" Tiara was thinking when the discussion about beverages was going to end.

"Coffee gets me dehydrated easily", Scarlett had a large sip.

Tiara looked around the large windows. The view, stunning as it was the day before, reminded her how overwhelmingly beautiful her city was. Sun was shining at the top creating glitters on the Thames water. Towards the western corner of the view tall glass buildings were reflecting sunlight. It was a bright day, for now.

Scarlett placed the saucer and cup on the table, folded both hands together tightly and leaned forward, "Tell me Tiara, did you find Damien?"

Tiara smiled a little, "You are looking relaxed Scarlett. It's a good sign. You are recovering"

"Thank you. I was in good hands. Doctor did a good job. I slept like a log last night"

"That's good. That's good", Tiara stood up, "I'm sorry I just can't sit at once place, like many other things I can't do well"

Scarlett joined the muted laughter that came from Tiara.

Tiara continued, "Did you ever go to Damien's home? Or … you just had the address from him?"

Scarlett nodded thoughtfully, "He had given me the address, I don't remember when, probably when we were publishing his book"

"The thing is, he doesn't live there. It's a fake address"

"What?" Scarlett gasped.

"He lied to you. In all sorts of ways. A, his address is fake. B, his phone number. It's a pay as you go phone. He simply trashed the SIM"

Tiara stared at Scarlett who was still a statue with her mouth open.

"Have another sip, Scarlett. You had befriended an imposter"

"I just can't believe", She picked up the cup and had a sip.

"There are quote a lot of Damien Andersons in town", Tiara continued, "but none of them match this man. And… one more thing, he is not even from South

Africa. Embassy has no record of him migrating in the last thirty years, or embassy records could be awfully wrong"

Scarlett was staring with bewilderment.

"Do you know why he did that? Why did he lie to you so much? What did he want?"

Scarlett exhaled deep, "I have no clue. I'm mortified. I suppose he wanted my money, but he could have asked me. I was always ready to help him"

"Yes. His book publisher confirmed that you did everything for him"

Scarlett paused for a second, looked into Tiara's eyes and said, "So you inquired there?"

"It's part of the investigation. I've also spoken to Nadira"

"Nadira, who?" Scarlett curled her eyebrows.

"Do you... ", Tiara strolled by the window. She was relishing the power of investigation. For once at least, she was feeling like she had control of a situation, "Remember anyone named Jamal?"

"Jamal...", Scarlett looked pensive, as if trying to recollect something.

"Nadira is an Arabic woman living in the house matching your Damien's address. She claims that you befriended her partner, Jamal. Not only you, but also a group of friends of yours. You and your friends... were working to help Jamal out of his financial condition. He had some dreams of staging a play, something like that. Do you think Nadira is speaking the truth?"

Scarlett sighed, had another sip, and placed the cup on the saucer. Then she removed her glasses, rubbed both eyes with the tip of her fingers, put the glasses back on and said, "It's a sad story. Jamal was trying hard against oppression. People were shackled by obscure labor companies and the government of those places never took any action. The world needed to know that. He was guilty...although nothing was his fault, of not being able to help his people...for living far away from them. He decided to speak up using a play. I met him through a friend. We have a group of friends, that's right. One of them introduced me to Jamal. We wanted to help him. It's not that we have anything against any nation by any means. It's about helping oppressed people. We tend to do that. Help anyone oppressed... we come across...men, women, children. Sometimes..."

"Who's we?"

"The group of my friends. They are from different backgrounds working in different professions, all sharing a common goal to stand by oppressed people. There's no color or religion or gender or nationality of an oppressed person. It's circumstantial"

"Impressive"

"But why is it important? Jamal is long gone. He committed suicide. We were devastated when that happened. We still miss him. Why are you dragging him into this?"

"You tell me Scarlett. Why did your partner give you an address which belongs to your old friend's partner? What's the connection there?"

"I don't know", Scarlett was brusque, "I don't know this person by name Nadia. I never met anyone like that. Damien was up to something for sure, but I don't know what that was"

"That's where we are right now. We have no trace of Damien. All we have is a set of characters. I have verified Jamal's case history and it's correct that he committed suicide last year in the month of June. So, I guess, we'll just have to search more and find Damien"

"Hmmm", Scarlett leaned back on the sofa and folded her legs up. Tiara noticed patches of golden hair all around her bare legs. Scarlett wasn't as groomed as Nadira was, concluded Tiara.

"Do you know what I'm thinking?" Scarlett asked thoughtfully.

"I don't"

"I am thinking…is this going anywhere by any means? Well…I agree…Damien committed a crime by hitting me. Perhaps…perhaps… he did try to kill me.

But, at the same time…he was enraged. He had temper issues. If I had problems with that, I should have left him. He didn't have money and had constantly asked me for help. If I didn't like him doing that, I should have been gone. But I didn't leave him. Because… deep inside… somewhere, I knew that he loved me", Scarlett rested head backwards on the sofa, looking upwards to the ceiling, "It's a shame that it turned out ugly. I told him an awful lot of nasty stuff. He lost it completely. I now regret you know, I shouldn't have said all that, to anyone, let alone my boyfriend"

As Scarlett paused, Tiara said, "And…what do you want me to do about it?"

"I think…I think I am… going to withdraw this case"

"Withdraw?" Now it was Tiara's turn to be surprised.

"That's what I'm thinking. It doesn't make any sense for me to punish him like this. It's already broken between us. He's never going to come back to me. And I'm not going to find him either. No one is at loss. I suffered a trauma, but I'm over it now, thanks to all the care you guys have taken. I don't think I want to hunt him down and put into jail"

"Alright", Tiara sighed, "Alright…If that's what you want. I'm not entirely sure what the process is, you might have to contact the office. It could be a long one"

"I shall do that. Most certainly. I'm sorry to disappoint you Tiara", Scarlett said apologetically.

"I am not disappointed. It's entirely your choice. I just think he violated the law and should be brought to justice"

"I know I know. But at the same time, I still love him. I can't do that. There is no point of crying over spilled milk. It was all my fault"

"I understand," Tiara nodded. She paused for a second and said "Right then. I should get going. It was nice working with you"

Scarlett stood up and walked behind Tiara towards the door. After Tiara exited the door, she looked back at Scarlett who was standing by the door. Scarlett said with a smile, "You know what? I think we could be friends. We should catch up sometime. After work maybe? With a drink?"

Tiara smiled halfheartedly. A gloomy disappointment of closing the case was biting her. Just less than ten minutes ago, she was proud of herself being able to communicate with command. Like all other times, her joy took no time to disappear. She managed to say with quite an effort, "I'll think about it. You have a good rest of your day Scarlett"

7

Three months later, on a sunny late Spring afternoon, Tiara was walking around the docklands, towards the high-rise buildings, in her faded blue jeans and gray tee that printed two eggs at the front side, meticulously ironed last night. The new shoe, that she had purchased at discount last week, was shining at her feet and the gold bracelet that Barbara had gifted her on her fifteenth birthday, was hanging loose at her wrist. She looked fresh, after a good sleep and hot bath and lighter shades of makeup on her face.

Afternoons are always busy in this part of the city as hundreds of people step out for lunch, around the food stalls or the take-away restaurants. A large queue in front of the mobile creperie reminded Tiara that she hadn't tasted crepe for a very long time. Many such small pleasures of life had been evading her for the last few years, including the pandemic years. Counting in her mind, she realized that she hadn't visited a new place or had any holiday trips, hadn't watched a film in the cinemas while eating popcorn, hadn't been drunk enough and of course there was no love in her life.

Tiara had left the Met volunteer job after the case was withdrawn. It was her sixth attempted profession to find something meaningful out of her life. When she was a waitress, a constant fear about her manager used to accompany her. He was a difficult man and always demanded more hard work. The job lasted only three weeks before Tiara left the restaurant weeping to herself. The next job was a receptionist at a spa. Once again, the old lady owner of the spa was mean to everyone. She yelled at Tiara for every mistake and after the third mistake Tiara's confidence had hit the rock bottom. Then the next job was assisting an attorney. The man with patches of gray hairs, who was one of the partners in the firm, worked late in the evening preparing real estate contracts where Tiara helped with typing and formatting on the computer. One evening he asked Tiara to massage his aching shoulders. Tiara was happy to assist. Soon his requests became frequent and eventually one day he demanded Tiara must devote more of her service. Her last job was at the home of an online reel creator, who focused on cheat dramas where a cheating incident between a couple gets busted within the short period of time allocated for the video. The reel maker was a young man with long hair and drank RedBull very frequently standing on his balcony. He and his girlfriend were the primary actors and Tiara would occasionally appear in the video, to shake the audience's attention when they were about to get distracted and thinking of scrolling up. Video creations were painstakingly long. The man would spend hours editing the multiple copies of the same while Tiara would wait patiently browsing her phone. During the pandemic, the man demanded more hours as more people came into the online video world. Tiara spent long hours but did not receive the cash money promised. When she requested the payment, the couple argued that they could find anyone doing her job.

She could never overcome such constant uneasiness while working with someone else. It was like a fear that had no name; a fear that was ingrained in her mind from her own neighborhood when she was young, along with a few other girls who loved to have all the fun at her expense. Those girls, now women, had moved on and dispersed to different parts of the country. But their shadows still loomed over Tiara's mind. They continued appearing in ghastly forms when she was alone, even in her sleep. They are like shadows, laughing at her at first and then taking different shapes of the girls, of Jasmine, of Martha and of Myriam. The largest shadow had always been in the form of Stella. Even in her dream, Tiara could feel her feet cold and shivering; and her palms sweating. Those shadows took her stuff away, like her only favorite little white squishy toy puppy and her multicolored ball; they forced her to run around the ground, laps after laps. Then Stella pulled her up from the ground as if she was just a puppet, and quickly switched her upside down by catching her legs in two hands. Tiara screamed and cried but other shadows rolled on the ground with joy. One of them threw some dust on Tiara's face. Tiara thought she would go blind. She screamed in agony. She could see her mum's shadow coming closer. The shadow listened to her complain. Did she listen at all? Tiara was not sure. Mum looked sleepy. Her eyes were red. She sipped from a glass. What was she drinking? In another dream Tiara was going to school. She walked with everyone else. Stella's shadow pushed Tiara on the road and Tiara almost fell under the bus. Tiara looked up. It was bus number twenty-five. The driver screamed at Stella, but she just giggled and walked away. When Tiara woke up, the nightmare and reality appeared to have merged. Tiara's mind was telling her that in her real life, the bus incident had certainly taken place. Dreams were merely reflecting her real life.

Tiara stood near the crepe counter and inhaled deeply. It felt intoxicating. Though she already had eaten at home, she thought she could eat a crepe, maybe just one, but the queue was too long to cross. She didn't have so much time. Jacob would be waiting. Tiara looked at her watch and started walking to the building at the opposite side of the road. She was supposed to go to the tenth floor.

Jacob was in her school. He was one of the very few people who had never intimidated her. It could be because Jacob himself was a shy and loner boy or it could also be that he had a soft corner for Tiara. Soon they became good friends. Some days, Jacob used to buy ice cream for Tiara with the money he had earned by pleasing his parents by completing chores at home. Tiara loved Jamoca-Almond from Baskin Robbins and Jacob indulged her occasionally with that. Jacob had curly hair and a thick pair of lips. He was bigger than Tiara in size and often other children stayed away from them because of his size.

Jacob maintained his friendship with Tiara strongly even after many years of graduation. He was admitted to a university in the north-west and eventually returned with a degree in journalism. While he was studying Tiara went to her college in south London. They spoke over the phone, chatted, shared pictures, emotions and laughter. Jacob was an ambitious man who had a dream of growing in a career, to achieve a meaningful living from his passion for journalism while Tiara, had no direction or any clear vision on what her next few years of graduation would have looked like. Jacob was affable and self-assured; many people were fond of him. He found the love of his life from a pub while Tiara was being heartbroken multiple times. Jacob married Rachel a few years ago while Tiara was still trying to date online. Rachel liked Tiara when they first met, and the feeling was mutual. At first, Tiara thought Rachel was a wise woman not only because she spoke elegantly about every subject but also, she was from an academic family with both parents being professors. She was warm and sensitive. Tiara tried to find more friends in Jacob's circle, but she was inhibited and awkward of herself in front of them. The men in the circle wore shiny suits, had gel in their hair, drank champagnes from thin flutes and played golf as a hobby. The women spoke about politics, history and stock markets. They were eloquent, confident and competitive. She started maintaining a safe distance from all of them and eventually from Jacob.

Jacob was waiting in the lobby. He wore a light blue shirt well tucked on a black trouser. The identity card tag was hanging over his neck. After a long warm hug Tiara had to register her name in the reception and soon, they were inside the cafeteria. When they sat on a table by the window with cups of coffees, Tiara was admiring Jacob's life in her mind. A famed news agency office at the high-rise modern towers at the most economically vibrant part of the town; what else was remaining?

"You look great and successful", Tiara exclaimed.

Jacob smiled heartily, "I am not successful. Still struggling."

"Are you?"

"I am. Trust me. Everyone struggles in my profession. There's never a moment you can relax. I enjoy what I do. And that's a satisfaction"

"Well said. That's what matters the most. How's Rachel?"

"She's doing great. Guess what, we're going to be parents in the next two months", Jacob's eyes glittered.

"Are you? Oh my god", Tiara closed her mouth with both her hands while shades of tears appeared at the corner of her eyes. She was genuinely happy for Jacob who, Tiara always had thought, was going to be a great father. Many times, Tiara wondered she would be a terrible mother, not only because she was still not settled, but also the fact that she could not teach her child any wisdom other than instructing to stay away from bullies.

"I'm so happy for you", Tiara stood up and hugged Jacob again.

"Save some for Rachel too", Jacob patted her at the back, "When are you visiting us? Rachel will be very excited if you come to see her"

"I am going to. Very soon", She wiped the corner of her eyes with the back of her palms. Jacob noticed that but ignored silently.

Tiara was unable to speak with emotion. Jacob let her settle down. She pulled her hair from both sides to the back pretending to tie them together.

"So tell me about you Tiara, what are you up to?", Jacob sipped the coffee.

"Me? Oh, it's just as usual. I wanted to see you because… I really need some help from you. I don't want to spoil the happy mood, perhaps we can discuss it another time"

"Are you out of your mind? Did I ever not listen to you when you had a problem?"

"I know. You have…always been there. But this time, you are so happy, you are…going to be a father, I just … don't want to overload you with all nagging problems of my life"

"Cut the crap Tiara, what is it? Are you running out of money?"

"Well, that too. But most importantly, I need a job. I

need to do something. It's been three months and I have nothing to do. I tried watching reels, binge watched Netflix, cooked for a few days but nothing helped. I even worked at a Tesco just for a day to see how it felt. It sucks. My life, my surroundings, there's nothing to motivate me", Tiara was almost diving into a depression.

She looked away to the window to ensure no tear was leaking out. It was still mildly sunny outside, quite contrary to her mood.

"Go on Tiara, I'm listening", Jacob's tone reminded her of childhood.

"First of all, I have to say sorry to you for not meeting for a year. Is it a year already?"

"It's in fact a little more than that.", Jacob grinned.

"I know you were mad at me. But believe me, I really wanted to go to the party. I just couldn't arrange the money I needed. I couldn't afford Majorca. It was too much for me. I was jobless. I was broken. Mum could have helped but you know, I would not ask her back then…"

"You could've asked me", Jacob interrupted her.

"No Jacob. I could not. You have a family. You have responsibilities. Besides, there were a whole bunch of other people from your circle. What would I tell them? Jacob sponsored me? When would I pay you back? You know Jacob, if something I have learnt from my life, at all, is to accept my situation and carry on. Some of us are not just lucky enough. For me, it's even worse… every day I'll have to think about what I should be doing tomorrow…every day is a struggle. I'm happy when I work initially but then it turns out to be the same. Always. Can you believe it? It happens every single time"

"You don't like the job?"

"Not always. I liked the Met job. It wasn't a job but volunteering…I could have worked hard on it…and eventually applied for a real job. Or could have been a detective"

"Then why did you leave?"

"I couldn't handle James. A colleague of mine. He tried to suppress me. Ordered me as if I was his assistant. It happens all the time. I meet bullies. In all my jobs. They drive me crazy. I hate that moment when someone takes control over me. It's the same familiar feeling. I had it since childhood… and never really got over it… never…I tried a lot…but no luck. I'm always landing into a wrong job where wrong people are waiting for me"

Jacob sighed and placed his hand on Tiara's shoulder, "And what makes you think that you are not going to find a bully in a job you are asking for?"

"I don't know", Tiara held her head with both hands, "Do you have a job for me? Anything will do? Even a photocopier in your office. I want to get out of home every morning and come back in the evening. I need to get engaged in something. Do you have a job?"

"I need to check Tiara. I think I might have something, but I can't promise. My editors are looking for a new story, something out of the box. If you are able…to produce something like that, even if you don't have a degree…well, I think we could manage that, we could put you through many training sessions, but the first part is tricky, can you write?"

"Write as in?"

"You need to be able to find a story and then write it. I can help you with the writing, but it needs to be original. And the story part of it…is the most important. The editorial board must like it"

Tiara thought for a moment, "When do you need a story…of that sort?"

"Anytime. Sooner the better. The position is open, and we are trying through internal referrals first. Just one thing"

"Yes?" Tiara was not able to blink. It was a huge ask from Jacob. Finding an exciting story that can feature in a newspaper? How could she even think of something like that? She came here to ask for a clerical job at the most. This was beyond all imaginations.

"The pay will be less as the position will be confirmed only after a year of apprenticeship"

"I'll be more than happy with that", Tiara took both of Jacob's hands into her two hands, "I'm just looking to work"

"All good then. Start looking for a story. I shall put the word with the editor. But…"

Tiara stayed motionless allowing Jacob to continue.

"Tell me about the bully part. How will you solve that? What if you quit this job too? It's going to be embarrassing for me"

"I know. That's why I'm going to be extremely careful. I've quit six times already. I hate that feeling. I hate myself, but I just can't get away from the bullies at work. But I promise you Jacob, nothing like that will happen this time. I may die but will never let you down"

"Well, in most jobs like mine, there are bullies and gaslighting, but there are also policies to overcome them. You will have to make the right decision at the right time. Whether you want to keep the trouble suppressed or bring it up to the authorities and make it open and dirty"

"Yeh. I heard about these things. When I was working at the attorney office, I could have complained about it to the other two partners, but I was afraid. I decided to leave instead. Should never have done that"

Tiara looked at her watch, "Am I wasting a lot of

your time? I think I should leave now. Your lunch time must have been over long back"

"But I still have loads to catch up on. What about we meet sometime for dinner at my place? You could meet Rachel and her baby bum"

"That sounds great", Tiara swallowed. Then she stood up, "Just text me when, and meanwhile…"

"You find your story. That's the first thing"

8

Talking to Jacob was always refreshing for Tiara. He was sensitive, attentive and wise. The best part was, he had always encouraged Tiara to speak up, no matter what the content was. Being a single child without any cousins or male relatives, Tiara had no exposure to men until she went to school. That was the beginning of their friendship, and it continued forever. Naturally, Jacob was not an all-purpose male figure. Tiara indeed, missed having a father in many ways, including the days, when a father of her school friend came for pickups, or she noticed a father being at home during a playdate. Tiara wanted to understand the feeling of a third person at home; a loud male presence. Barbara used to say that Tiara's father had a big mustache and thick long hair. He spoke in a loud voice. And that was all the memory she could preserve. There was no story about him, no photograph, no letter; not even a single object that could have been associated with him. He was just never there; nonexistent. Barbara never explained why her father had left. Tiara didn't want to know. She had built her world without a father. Barbara was everything in that world. Barbara worked hard at the hospital, cooked during breaks, chased Tiara for homework and drank when she was alone. Tiara had never seen tears in Barbara's eyes. They were large black eyes, covered behind a tiny glass that helped her see from a distance clearly. Sometimes, those eyes were too dry to be true. They stared at the void, behind the small window from the kitchen, that overlooked a tiny part of the sky above. Barbara lived in solitude. She had no friends besides two women from the neighborhood.

When Tiara was very young, they lived with her grandparents. Tiara had no memories but Barbara sometimes narrated stories of how her grandmother put her to sleep at night. Barbara said her grandparents went back to Jamaica and consequently, they moved to a council home. When Tiara asked why they had to go back but Barbara had no answer. At many other instances, Barbara failed to provide satisfactory answers to Tiara's questions. During those awkward moments, Barbara would turn her eyes away or pay attention to her phone or just walk away. One of the very few people Barbara spoke to, was the woman from the next door. She was a good help to look after Tiara during the long work hours. There were days when Tiara had to complete homework at the next door, or even sleep there because Barbara had night duties. Next day, she was fed breakfast and sent to school as if it was her second home. When she came back in the afternoon, the door would stay open. Barbara could be spotted near the kitchen, cooking without a light turned on. She preferred darkness. The pot on the hob would continue snuggling the low flame for hours and Barbara would not pay any attention to it. Tiara would pull out a glass from the cupboard, decorated by her collection of Peppa Pig stickers. At the cracking sound of the old cupboard, Barbara would turn around and smile. Tiara would try to look for a drop of tear, but the eyes would remain dry. Barbara would turn off the stove, pick up a bottle of colorless liquid and a glass from the top corner rack and walk to her bedroom. Much later, Tiara realized that the bottles had labels that spelled Smirnoff. Tiara would follow her to the door. Barbara, sitting at the edge of the bed, would pour the liquid in the glass. Staring at Tiara she would smile and say,

"How was your day?"

Tiara wished she could tell her stories of her school, how she played pirates with two other girls, how she enjoyed the ballet class or planned for the next field trip fun with Jacob. Instead, she would draw a blank. She hated those uneasy moments. She knew that Barbara would soon close the door, leaving her no choice, but to face her tormentors waiting at the front yard for another fun day at her expense. Tiara wished she could stay longer talking to her mum; she just wanted to talk, anything that came to her mind. One day she said,

"Why do you have to work so hard?"

Barbara laughed and said in a whispering tone, "I need to earn money sweetie. How'll we eat if I don't work?"

"Miss Jones was saying, they don't pay you enough… but make you work a lot"

Barbara laughed again, "Are you talking to her about my work? Are you?"

"I did. She also said…Harlem Street…", Tiara tried to recollect," has better clinics where they pay more"

"Harley Street", Barbara corrected.

"Yes, Harley Street. Why don't you go there…mum?"

"Did she also tell you what kind of nurse they need?"

"What kind nurse are you mum?"

"Theater Support"

"What's Theater Support?"

Neighborhood girls were ganged up before she even stepped out of her home. They were not only older than her but also stronger. On the very first day Tiara had realized that she would have to go through a difficult time to break into the group. Stella had already announced that Tiara had a ugly hair. Tiara did not remember when her mother made her hair last time. Stella often pulled the end of the hair tightly with her fist making Tiara scream in agony; then Stella let it go causing Tiara to fall on the ground at the recoil. They despised her hair as much as they despised her overall. The girls made her run around to fetch the ball every day when they played tennis or soccer. Failure to do so, would result in an hour-long timeout, locked behind the wooden doors of Mrs. Jenkin's storeroom. Tiara hated the room; it was dark and smelled foul. She would cry hard and sometimes someone from the Jenkins family would open the door, yelling at her asking why she stepped into the room. Tiara wished her school lasted longer. Some of her friends from School went to dance or swimming classes after hours but Tiara had to sit in the bus and wait for the tormenting afternoon. When her mum had different duty hours, her key would be hidden behind the door mat. Barbara told her there was nothing to steal from the house. Even if it was kept open no one would break in. Tiara knew that Barbara had prepared snacks that were arranged in the fridge. Tiara also knew how to use the microwave to warm it up.

Some days, she wanted to stay inside, hidden in her bedroom. The small bed made of black wood and matching dresser by the side of it, often gave warmth of a hideout. She would spend the afternoon placing the stickers on the body of the dresser. After an hour she would lose her sanity. It was hard to stay inside, especially during the summer afternoons with humidity creeping inside the room. Tiara would try focusing on something else. Some other days, she would color her lips with Barbara's lipstick from the drawer; another day, draw funny shapes on the mirror with it or spread the face powder on the dresser table and create figures through it. Long afternoons still wouldn't end with even longer evenings waiting behind. Finally, she could not avoid stepping out and asking the gang whether she could join them. Stella often wore a yellow frock that ended at her knees. She tied a red belt at the center of her body and a red head band on her head. When she spoke, Tiara shivered. When she pushed Tiara to the ground Tiara thought the world would end. Soon, she appeared in Tiara's nightmare and that was the beginning of Tiara's misery. Now their shadows were at home as well, in her sleep and in her bed.

Tiara wanted to leave the neighborhood. She discussed her condition with Jacob at school and he showed tremendous support. Jacob advised her to talk to elders about it. When she told the next-door woman whether the gang could be tamed, the woman just shrugged saying that they were all children and children must solve their own problems. One day, at school, her teacher spoke about a behavior called bullying and how everyone must be aware of it. After the class, Tiara spoke to the teacher about her own example. The teacher suggested a meeting with her mum.

Spirited, Tiara went home with a wide smile. It was one of those days, when the door was open, and Barbara was opening the drink.

"Mum, my teacher wants to talk to you"

Barbara looked sharply at her, "What have you done?"

"I haven't done anything. I swear"

"Then why does she want to see me?"

"I told her how the girls here bully me every day. She wants to discuss with you"

"Which girls bully you?"

"Stella… and others. But mostly Stella", Tiara said pensively.

"Do you know what bullying means? I don't think these girls are bad. They are just playing with you"

"I don't want to stay here mum. The girls are mean. I don't like them. I want to go somewhere else", Tiara demanded.

"We can only afford so much, sweetie. We need to save some money for your future. We can't spend it on a rented house"

"Why don't you join the Harley Street clinics?"

Barbara smiled, "You are not going to leave that are you?"

"I heard they pay really...really good. There are old white doctors with gray hair. They are wise and rich"

"Now you are talking like a racist"

"What's a racist?"

The little play area near the front yard would get covered with autumn leaves from the trees around the street. The late evening sun behind the next door would create a silhouette and decorate the scattered leaves with different shapes of shadow. When it drizzled in the afternoons of Spring and Summer, children rushed for the old slide. They loved sliding in the rain. And winter would occasionally shower it with light snow, so light that Tiara would imagine someone accidentally sprinkling her mum's face powder everywhere. On Christmas eve, all the families around the street gathered to listen to the Carol. Barbara would smile at others but keep herself reserved. Women, with their hair washed neatly, faces brushed with light make-up and wearing colorful skirts, would be chatty, talking about families and friends and people they knew. Men, wearing new suites and shiny black shoes, would speak about soccer and council politics. Tiara loved to listen to those men and women. She loved those moments, to be hidden among people; a moment, not claimed by anyone in particular.

Christmas ended, then came the new year. There was just one New Year's Eve when Barbara took her to watch the fireworks by the Thames. She stood in the line that lasted for hours. At the end of it, she cried of an aching leg and promised that she would never want to see the fireworks again. The very next year's eve was lonely as Barbara had duty that night. Tiara spent the evening watching television at her dining table. The next new year was quiet too and again an evening in front of the television. Years passed by. The autumn leaves arrived, followed by powder snow and then followed by drizzles and rains. Tiara grew up. So did the girls and Stella. Tiara could see them less and less. Barbara had relaxed her rules on television. Tiara spent a lot of hours in front of it. She realized that the other girls must have been doing the same. When Barbara bought her first phone, a new world opened up in front of her. There was no need to look at the television anymore. There was no need to even step out. Stella and the girls were out of school and some of them had moved out to different colleges. Stella was going to a local college but was busy with her own life. Only time Tiara would encounter her, was at any block party or nights like Christmas eve. She would turn her eyes down even though Stella would push or nudge from behind to remind her who the boss was. Tiara made friends online. She was gladly comfortable with her secluded life. Her world was no longer tied to the bullies she hated so long. She was happy that there were no bullies online, until there were. The day when someone left a nasty comment on her post, she cried in the bathroom. Then she realized that, more and more people whom she thought of as online friends, had started being mean to her posts. Soon, she reduced her posts and videos, and unfriended some people. Meanwhile, the real world moved on. Barbara grew older. Tiara noticed gray hair on her head and folds in her skin. She reduced drinking and was spending more time on her phone. Tiara had no idea what Barbara would be doing on the phone. She could be chatting with someone. A friend?

Likewise, a year later, Tiara came across Alice, in a match providing app. It was not the first time she was attracted to a girl but right after the first date, she was convinced that Alice was going to win her completely. Alice radiated energy, in whatever she did. She was confident, sometimes arrogant and eccentric too. Her attire matched her energy. She had straight silky hair, used glossy eyeshadows and lipsticks and wore a nose ring. There was a gold locket in the shape of the Empire State Building of New York hanging from her neck. Alice told stories about places she had visited, one among them was New York. Alice lived alone, while studying in the university. She told stories of what the meaning of free life was. Tiara considered her cool and wanted to match her. She would spend hours in Debenham at Oxford Street selecting something that could match Alice. She would buy a red tight and rainbow loose top that flowed till the knee. She had never spent that much time on her own before. Alice had made it happen; as if a new life was brought to Tiara. They went swimming together. Tiara started paying attention to her health. She worked out longer, switched to skinny latte and drank more water. She wanted to glow, look healthier and beautiful.

Soon, it was time she confessed near Barbara about her choice of partner. She had been avoiding the moment for quite some time, but Alice wanted her to come out clean. And, thus, Tiara, stood near the door of the bedroom where Barbara was resting on the bed while looking at her phone.

"Mum, I need to tell you something"

Tiara thought she would avoid any dramatic reaction by directly jumping into the point, but it did not go as planned. Barbara refused to believe that Tiara was able to make any decision about her sexuality.

"Why do you think I don't know what I am?"

"Because you are a child. I am your mother. I know you more than you know yourself"

"I'm not a child anymore. And I know what I actually am. I love Alice. And that's how I am"

"You don't love her. You don't even know what love is. You can't love a girl. It can't happen that way"

"Grow up mum. Look around. It's everywhere. I'm not the only one"

"It's not everywhere. It's a fad. A fantasy. Rich women's pass time. We don't do that"

"Mum…you are disgusting. You sound like a…"

"In God…I believe…and in his doctrine"

"And what exactly is that?"

Soon the day arrived, when after endless arguments about humanity, sexuality and God, Barbara announced the verdict that anyone staying in her home must obey her rules. On that day, Tiara, with swollen eyes and broken voice, declared that she could find her own way without any trouble. Tiara was out of the home with just one suitcase where she had managed to pack everything, she thought belonged to her. Beside clothes there were only necessary items like toothbrush, sanitary napkins, comb, cosmetics, phone charger, paracetamol and few pairs of shoes. She was starting a new life, with as few as possible strings attached to the previous one. Sitting in the bus when she realized that she was not going to return, tears covered her entire cheeks. She was trying to convince herself that her mother's act was not bullying but an impulsive decision. After a long bus ride when she reached Alice's apartment, she was able to gather parts of her strength back. Alice's love and affection cheered her up quickly. Soon, they were baking together in the kitchen, walking around the park in the neighborhood, making love on the floor, and watching movies late at night.

Alice had a large circle of friends from the university and other sources. Tiara was able to befriend them easily. After a few weeks of exhausting late nights and throw ups in the bathroom, it dawned on Tiara that she was still a student who needed to complete the university and more importantly, her savings were about to finish. Alice was able to get her a job at the Frankie and Benny's nearby with the help of a friend. Job hours made Tiara's life difficult. She had to work in the evenings until the restaurant was closed. Then Alice would take over for some more hours of enjoyment. When she woke up in the morning with a heavy head and burning throat, there would be no time to look at the study. Workload at the college started to take a toll on her too. Restaurant manager's unhappiness started to increase. When the manager issued multiple warnings, a familiar feeling started to grow inside her. She felt dominated and bullied; yet again. And consequently, her confidence dipped, and fear climbed high. Consecutive three sleepless nights convinced her to quit the job. Being bullied again was the last thing she could accept. When she returned home that evening, to her disappointment, Alice resented her on why she could not focus on the job more. That was the first night when Alice avoided touching her and turned her face towards the wall. Weeping silently in the darkness, Tiara felt that she was missing her mum; the lullabies Barbara used to sing after drinking vodka, her bedroom's comfort and her neighborhood's noise.

Alice was normal the very next day, but Tiara could not be the same anymore. Her monetary situation started to decline sharply. She tried for similar job applications but realized that for every job there were too many candidates. There was no shortage of cheap labor. Media blamed the influx of people from Europe; some policy makers started to demand a new world out of Europe; people argued in social media endlessly about the good and the bad sides of the current system, while Tiara started losing hopes and getting indebted to Alice more and more. The city turned a deaf ear on her. Endless labyrinth of streets could not guide her to any employment. Her weekends had changed. They would start with Tiara rushing in the morning to the addresses she had already collected from the employment advertisements. After a long day of struggle when she was back Alice would have already gone to some party. Tiara would weep in the bathtub or eat an ice cream that Alice had bought for her. If she stared out of the window, she would only see the dark clouds preparing for the next lashes of rain.

Alice insisted she could help find something. One day, she took Tiara to a tiny block at the southern part of the city. A small yard, consisting of five homes without any touch of adequate sunlight, was their destination. Tiara heard stories about desperate girls taking desperate steps during desperate times, but she trusted Alice more than anyone else. Though the house looked like a set from a criminal film and the man opening the door had a vibe of all possibly horrendous activities, Tiara was still hoping that it was not what it had looked like. When they were taken into a room where a man stood behind a camera and another man tried to explain something to Alice, Tiara screamed at Alice demanding an explanation.

"Listen honey, this pays like a jackpot. You can't match this anywhere. All we have ...", Alice could not finish as Tiara screamed at her,

"How could you think I was going to do this?"

"Why not? I did it before. It wasn't too bad"

Tiara was fuming, "You are out of your mind. I'm not what you think I am", She started walking out of the room while Alice blocked the door with hands stretched and said in a tone as if she was chewing her own words, "Listen Tiara, we don't have much choice. You don't have any money. You haven't found a job yet. What are you going to do?"

"I'm not doing this. I'd rather die", Tiara tried to push Alice.

"Don't be silly Tiara. This is safe. We're not going to sleep with anyone. It's just us. We're going to be ourselves, like how we are in our own bed. They're just going to film us. They'll pay you well. Trust me. We can be happy again", Alice spoke in a gentle voice.

"Leave me alone. You are a tart…but I'm not", Tiara pushed Alice aside and started walking. Alice pulled her right hand strongly and with a twist brought her down to her knees. Tiara groaned in agony. Alice held her chin with her right hand and frowned, "Listen to me Tiara. You're going to have to do what I say. You owe me a lot. You are a piece of shit… you're living in a shithole. I'm the one who showed you how to live. Now you fucking call me tart. I'm going to show you what a tart means"

Tiara pushed Alice's hand out and stood on her feet. She looked at the room where both men were patiently waiting. It appeared as if people there had experienced such quarrels before. Tiara looked into Alice's eyes and said with a strong voice, "Now you listen to me. You... don't bully me. Nobody... bullies me. I'm a fucking free girl. I do what I fucking like..."

While walking out of the door, she realized that her relationship with Alice was all over. Without turning back, she strode as fast as she could to the bus stop. Sitting in the bus, she looked at the yard. There were no signs of Alice or the men. Her mind was empty like a piece of blank paper. Although she was glad to be safe, at the same time Alice's departure was creating chunks of pain in her chest. After an hour, she was out on the road with the same suitcase. Dark skies and growing intense rain signaled her that the next few hours were going to be miserable. It had to be the decision for existence. Tiara could not think of anything else. Sitting in the bus again, towards her home, she stared at the streets through the rain-soaked window. The city appeared like a ruthless dungeon where her first attempt to survive on her own turned out to be a failure. She wasn't equipped enough. When the bus was passing by the New Scotland Yard building, Tiara realized that she had a faint desire to work there. Perhaps, one day, she could live her dream.

Back home, she found Barbara standing in the kitchen; not particularly making anything but staring at a bowl in front of her. Hearing Tiara's footsteps, she turned her head. Again, Tiara could only see dry eyes and heavy lips. Barbara smiled warmly and said, "I was planning to make lasagna tonight. Glad that you came. It's your favorite. Let me get started".

Without saying another word, Barbara continued working in the kitchen for dinner while Tiara was able to hide herself in the bathroom for a marathon cry. The mother and daughter sat face to face at the dinner table. Barbara told her stories of how she was able to abandon alcohol completely with the help of yoga and meditation classes. Barbara looked pale under the ceiling lights of their room. She wasn't interested to know how Tiara lived while she was away or what happened with Alice. Barbara had moved on, physically and emotionally.

Next few days were busy as people from the neighborhood had plenty of questions. The woman next door was already aware that Tiara was a lesbian and that was why Barbara had thrown her out. Very soon, the news spread from her to everyone around. One day, Tiara found Barbara packing suitcases. To her surprise, Barbara said that they needed to move out as the neighbors were not pleased to live near a lesbian. Apparently, Stella was driving a movement for a cleaner neighborhood as she was expecting a child. Stella was ready to go to any extent to protect her children from any bad influence. Barbara was already prepared for this move, and she had finalized the new home as soon as Tiara returned. Still in shock, Tiara sat down on the floor while Barbara continued packing. They did not utter a word to each other until midnight when Barbara switched off the lights.

Following morning, they were in a taxi. Tiara was still trying to comprehend how quickly the world around her had turned estranged. Even in the era of modern gadgets and rapid scientific developments, few systems had hardly changed. The bully had finally won. She was able to displace Tiara, from her memories of childhood, adolescence and her roots.

Years went by. Tiara turned busy finishing university and thereafter trying to find a job. Since the incident with Alice and the displacement from the old home, Tiara's fear of bullies developed to an extreme. She could not tolerate anyone raising voice or ordering her to do something. Barbara was annoyed with her behavior. Under Barbara's pressure, Tiara had to visit therapy and medical consultations. Barbara named it Bully Allergy. Therapies were expensive and time consuming. Both mother and daughter agreed to postpone that until

Tiara was able to find a stable income. Years later, Tiara was still looking for that income at Jacob's office. When Tiara returned home after finishing lunch on that sunny spring day, Barbara was standing by the kitchen counter, trying to prepare something in a bowl.

"Are you making dinner?", asked Tiara, she was rejuvenated after meeting Jacob.

"I am going to. Soon. Tell me about Jacob. How is he doing?"

Tiara sat on the breakfast chair and stretched herself, "He works for a newspaper. He's smart as always. I think he'll become big very soon"

"Is he going to give you a job?"

"I wish he did. I've asked him already"

"You should have married him. You could have lived a different life…", Barbara looked at the bowl where she was mixing something while talking.

"Mum…"

"Yes I know I know. You don't like men. I know"

"He'll find me something. you don't worry"

"I hope it's soon. You know I am becoming old. I can't take care of you all the time. If you don't find anything at all, why don't you become a nurse? It's still not too late"

"Mum…remember what I said to you when you had asked me last time?"

"I don't remember. What did you say? Sometimes you are arrogant. You say things that I don't remember"

"I said…that…I didn't want to become like you"

"What's wrong with me?" Barbara raised her eyebrows.

"I don't want to end up drinking Vodka alone in my bed. It's too sad of a life"

"Really? Do you have any idea why I drank so much?"

"Because you were lonely. My father left you. There was no family. No friend. Why didn't you have a friend? Why didn't you marry again?"

"It's not about your father. I don't even remember him now. I never wanted to marry. Even if it was your father I wouldn't have married"

"So you like to live alone?"

Barbara opened the door of the oven, which was already heating up, dumped the mixture from the bowl into a baking tray and placed the tray inside. After closing the door of the oven, she turned to Tiara who was waiting patiently, and said,

"In nursing, I have seen lots of struggles, lots of blood. You have no idea how much that is…seen people dying…on the operation theater table. Some deaths are natural, like from a disease. A woman had cancer in her ears. She bled every day from her ears. Buckets full of blood. A colleague of mine worked on her. It was so much blood that…some days my colleague could not eat…because she could only see blood everywhere. When the woman died, we were relieved. But…there are other kinds of deaths which are more frightening. Often, we see patients coming in half dead, some stabbed from behind with the back half slit open, some smashed on the head with a fountain of blood flowing all over. I put them on the operation table. I dress their wounds, nurse them if they survive the night. These people are from different parts of the town, but they end up dying on the table. There are too many violent crimes at night. People, the young ones especially, in their twenties, die regularly. When I hear the stories about them, naturally, I thank God that we are still alive, but you know what bothers me the most?"

Tiara was listening intriguingly. She loved when Barbara spoke like that.

"What bothers me is the fact that…people could do such terrible things to each other. There's no compassion in this world. Everyone has forgotten all good things about being a human. When we go to church we learn mercy, kindness, empathy and so many other great things. But why do we not see them on the street? Why do these people forget what they had learned from Church or from their parents? I wish all religions just taught us one thing, that is not to hurt another person. And people could sincerely follow that…when I think about this, I feel you should stay away from this reality. I want you to be happy, even if you don't have a job or don't have a partner…you are still alive…that's the most important thing. When you say you don't want to be a nurse, I feel happy deep inside because I don't want you to experience what I have been doing years after years. Death is a terrible thing. Every time a young man died on my table I prayed for mercy from God. But my mind wouldn't listen to me. It wanted to rest. I drank Vodka"

Later at night, in bed, Tiara was thinking about the words Barbara said about religion. She was trying to remember where she had seen something similar. It was a book; written by someone called Damien, who went missing after assaulting his girlfriend. The one and only case she worked on and remained unsolved. Slowly, she moved to the closet where at the bottom row, she had affectionately packed her experience kits from the police life. The book was kept inside the packet. Surprisingly, she even had the bookmark in it, the old bill from Starbucks in Angel where she was reading the first few pages of it. She removed the bookmark aside. It started a new chapter.

THE FALL OF CLIVE

Day 1

My name is Clive. I am an acclaimed professor of History. Students from all over the country come to me for research and guidance. I often decide their futures, whether they like it or not. When I am not working, I like spending time reading with a glass of drink, sitting at my favorite pub. When I step out for a smoke, I leave my book folded with the bookmark in it. People speak to me at the pub casually. Some women approach me. They think I am attractive.

That's how I met Megan for the first time. When I was sitting with a drink she appeared from behind. She had brown hair and an enviable body. I thought she was half of my age. My only daughter had moved to Boston for higher studies. Megan looked only a little older than her.

The best part of Megan was that she was candid and

had no pretense. She asked me directly whether my name was Clive, and I was the professor she had thought I was. To my surprise, she told me that she had heard about me from a couple of her friends and wanted to meet me in person. I was already impressed with the elegant and soft-spoken nature of her. We discussed current affairs and some literature. She was well read; exactly the kind of woman I adored.

We decided to take a walk around the park. It was late in the evening and raining. I have never felt such a romantic vibe before. Wish we stayed longer but I had to return home to my wife. I wanted more of Megan.

Day 5

My wife had to go for a business trip. I realized that was my best chance. I phoned Megan to stay over with me. She was waiting for an evening like that. Soon, she arrived at the door with a small backpack full of her clothes. We were all prepared.

We opened a champagne bottle. I was unable to wait but Megan wanted it to be more graceful. She asked me to finish a shower while she arranged the room with a few lovely candles she had brought along. In all my previous occurrences, the encounters were direct without a single minute to think about the next step. Naturally,

I loved Megan's authentic style. When I came out of the bathroom, the room was decorated. Four candles were lit at four corners, the lights were switched off and on the center table, there was another candle beside the bucket and glasses. A melodious piano was being played using my Alexa. We were all set for the most romantic evening. We toasted the champagne to ourselves and finished the glasses at once. Within moments I heard my doorbell ring. It alerted me severely, but I assured myself that my wife was not going to return until the next afternoon.

When I opened the door, I saw a young man standing in front with an umbrella. I noticed it was raining outside. His face was covered with a covid mask. Before I asked his name, he told me he was my student, for many years. I could not recollect his name. The very next moment, I felt his face was turning blurred and the raindrops were turning thicker. I tried closing the door, but the man was holding it strong. I realized that my hands were weak, and my head was spinning. And immediately, like a flash, it all turned dark.

When I opened my eyes, it was still dark. My head was hurting, and my throat was sore. When I tried to touch my head, I realized that my hands were tied behind me together. So were my legs. I was shaking my whole body in sudden panic. With a couple of jerks, I toppled myself over on the floor. My elbow was hurt badly but I was on the ground. By moving my legs around, I realized that I was sitting on my toilet. It was my bathroom. Although it had a window there must have been darkness outside. How long was I senseless? I decided to turn the light on first. By dragging my body, I was able to reach the wall where the switches were. After a tremendous effort, I was able to pull myself up the wall to stand up and was able to press the switch with my mouth.

While trying to gather my thoughts I realized that Megan was obviously a con woman who got complete access to my home with her partner in crime, the man with the umbrella. I was blaming my libido for needlessly trusting a stranger so easily. She could have emptied the entire home by now. How will we ever find her or the man? The man wore a mask but had a large scar at the corner of his forehead. That could be useful for Police. I remembered a scar on someone before. Where did I come across such a scar? Was it a student? The man said he was a student for many years. Who was a student for many years? Suddenly it occurred to me who it was. The man was indeed an ex-student of mine. He never actually completed his degree as I was reluctant to proceed with him. Is this his revenge?

I started sweating from my head. If they wanted to rob me, why tie me in the bathroom? I will not be able to untie myself alone. The best I can do is to lie down on the floor waiting for my wife to rescue me. Meanwhile if I am thirsty, I can drink water from the tap. It will be a matter of little over twelve hours. Most people can survive that. But can I?

I looked around the door. It was a small bathroom. The window was tightly closed and faced a wall from the next house. This was the bathroom downstairs with no shower or tub in it. I cannot stay here for long, not even two hours because I have claustrophobia. When I go to work, I prefer driving or taking the bus to avoid going to the underground trains. I need air and most importantly an exit strategy. Underground trains are not at all well equipped with that. I even have trouble breathing when a flight took off or an elevator halted due to a fault. The simplest way to kill me was to lock myself inside a small room. I had joked about it many times in the past near my students. And he was there when I said it. He knew how to kill me. That was his plan. He wanted to kill me with the help of Megan.

Terrified, I looked around the bathroom. There is no way I can survive it. Even if my wife returned with an early flight by a miracle, I will be in trouble explaining to her why and how it happened, and investigation could expose my infidelity. I am going to lose everything even if I survive. They planned it well.

I never thought this was how my end was written, without any glory or any applause. I lived like an emperor but was dying like a wimp.

Goût de Lumiere meant strike of light. It is said that when undesired light triggers reactions inside the wine in a bottle, the wine starts tasting like a rotten vegetable. That's the reason wine is traditionally packed in dark bottles so that light could not reach it. Tiara had known the fact, since someone had explained to her in college, but could never taste the vegetable part in any wine. Was all wine she ever drank, kept in traditional bottles? How about the recent sparkling ones?

Trying to see through the sparkling liquid inside the glass in her hand, she wondered what type of bottle the wine had come from. Looking through liquid made the world in front her elongated, sometimes inflated. The sparkling liquid decorated parts of it with large bubbles that changed shape when the glass was turned from left to right or tilted towards the front. Looking through the liquid, the bartender, who had already introduced himself as John, with a wild looking beard, appeared inflated at the center of his body. Tiara giggled at her own childishness. Then she sipped from the glass, looked at the watch, browsed her phone occasionally, before convincingly concluding that it was indeed a bad idea to invite Scarlett for a drink.

Tiara had her number saved since the day of the case. Hesitating, in the beginning, she was able to dial her number last night. Scarlett's voice was warm and encouraging. Tiara expressed that she needed a favor to which Scarlett promptly agreed to meet at a place of Tiara's choice.

Tiara had arrived before time and indulged herself with a decent drink. Scarlett had mentioned that she would finish work early. Tiara hoped she was just late at work.

The pub was not overly filled up, but a sizable portion of the office crowd were present to enjoy drinks break. Atmosphere was overall elated. The jukebox was playing an old song where the singer wanted to be Grace Kelly but her looks were too sad and so he tried a little Freddie. Anticipating Scarlett's arrival, Tiara continued turning her head occasionally to the door, once, twice, thrice; she lost count soon but eventually, Scarlett arrived. Tiara, instantly adjusted herself straight on the barstool, pulled back the unstoppable hair from her forehead to back and took a deep breath. Scarlett looked heavier than last time. She had certainly gained more pounds which were visible beneath her purple sheath that ended at her knees. She had streaked parts of her hair purple which was left open to her shoulders. With her eyes wandering around the bar, Scarlett appeared busy and curious. After the initial warm hug, she positioned herself beside Tiara. As John arrived, Scarlett ordered a glass of champagne by indicating one with her index finger and Tiara noticed that Scarlett's nails were painted with red flower symbols on black base. Tiara had seen the symbol earlier in the form of a tattoo at the back of Scarlett's neck, on the last day of her investigation. Today, Scarlett appeared extremely tidy as compared to the days of investigation. She looked at Tiara with a large smile and said,

"So… how have you been Tiara? It was such a pleasant surprise"

"I know", Tiara returned the smile, "Last night, I was reading the book you had given me, and I just realized that you might be able to help me. Like I said, if it's of any trouble you can just ignore it"

"I'll be more than glad to help you with anything I can. I really liked you when you arrived for the investigation. I like strong women. You had it in you.

The power to drive something. Tell me how you have been. Are you still volunteering?"

"I had given up the police job…", Tiara lowered her eyes. It wasn't too often she had the opportunity to talk to another woman who is almost about her age. It was also not too often that anyone asked her whether she was employed. She moistened her upper lip with her tongue anticipating Scarlett to ask the next question.

"Why? What happened?" Scarlett asked.

"It didn't go as planned. My first case, which happened to be yours, failed. I was demoralized. On top of that, I was assigned a co-worker, the elderly gentleman who accompanied me that day…if you remember. His name is James. He bossed me completely. Every time he spoke to me it got on my nerves. I started to feel that he was bullying me. And I can't stand bullies. It drives me insane. I just couldn't handle it. So… I quit."

"That's sad. Really sad. People sometimes are so bossy…even when they are not the true boss"

"Tell me about you. What are you doing?" Tiara tried to remove the sympathetic focus from herself.

Scarlett smiled, "Me? I'm busy showing homes. Just kidding…I act busy…I'm actually…far from having to do anything. But I try to look tidy as if I'm going to an important meeting. Trust me, I'm the best-looking realtor in town. I'm the queen in my little office. They love me as a trophy, sitting at the corner and attending calls. I sometimes… do show homes but those days are rare…", Scarlett laughed out loud. Tiara smiled at her humility.

"Today, I wanted to leave at noon and my boss had nothing to say. I know they could get rid of me easily, but he has a soft corner for me. I think he'll never let me go. He probably expects some sort of work ethic from me which I don't have, I don't think I even know what that means. Sometimes, others just stare at me wondering, what on fucking hell this one is", Scarlett gulped a large volume from the glass and ordered one more. Tiara indicated she would top up as well.

"So here I am, at your service. You said you needed something. Tell me now. It's just me blabbering enough"

"Well, the thing is, when I was reading the book, I realized that the author had some strong views on bullying. In fact, the entire book is about bullying"

"That's so true", Scarlett shook her head from back to front by pressing her lips together. Her glasses moved front and back on her nose.

"What I exactly want is…a solution to my temperament. The thing is, I've had a rough childhood. I was bullied every day. There were few kids, all around my neighborhood. They were strong and ganged up against me. I had nightmares regularly of being beaten up by them and...in my real life...was also being thrashed every day. When I grew up...I realized that...I had no confidence. At every step, at the uni, at different workplaces, I feared people were bullying me. I was intimidated very easily. Is that a word for fear of being bullied? I have that. Do I look timid to you?"

"No no...", this time Scarlett shook her head from side to side, "You are not timid. Not at all. In fact, I felt you were strong when I saw you for the first time. How did you end up in the police if you had lack of confidence?"

"I wanted to overcome my fear. My mum said I was timid and shy. I could never handle tough guys. I wanted to prove everyone wrong. Believe me, I'd seen the Scotland Yard office only once from outside when I was young and that day, I had it in my mind. I wanted to be a cop. I worked hard for the volunteering job. But you see in the end, the bullies had full control over me. When I read this book, I started to hope that you could help me"

"I'm sorry about everything that happened to you Tiara. The worst of all is getting bullied in childhood. Imagine how hard it is for a young mind to handle such monsters. I can imagine what you had to go through all those years. How about now? Do you get some sort of mood swings or any kind of emotional breakdown? You don't have to tell me in detail. I'm only asking because you said, you get insane when you meet a bully"

"So far…I've rarely seen any emotional breakdown, but my mum could tell better. I think I'm …a bit of a wallflower….in general. Not too many people like me or hate me or even care about me. I…am mostly within myself. It's only…I can't control my mind when I meet one of those"

"Do you live with your mum?" Scarlett had a tiny sip while holding the flute with two fingers. Tiara observed the red flower again. It was a shiny piece of nail art. The black background was glossy and was reflecting its image on the flute.

"I live with my mum, yes. I've always lived with my mum. You know what, it's a pity…I completely agree. Girls of my age… certainly have better lives. I just couldn't manage to find a stable job", Tiara smiled tight.

"That's alright. It's not bad at all to stay with your mother. And talking about lives…look at mine…a complete meaningless piece of rubbish. You are much better, honestly"

"What are you talking about? What qualms do you have? You're rich, single, living a posh life, not caring about how much you get paid…what else is a better life?"

Scarlett smirked from the corner of her lips, "There's

always the dark side of the moon, my dear. This sweet little chum, quite often, turns into a sad monster. But we shall talk about that next time. Today, it's all about you. Tell me, what do you need me to do? I'm not a doctor or psychiatrist. You must have realized by now. Have you ever tried one by the way?"

"No I didn't. They are too expensive. And I wasn't sure whether I had any problem. In my society, people don't lie down on a beautiful leather couch to narrate their problems, but they learn to live with the problems"

"So, have you learnt to live with it?", Scarlett said with a sigh.

Tiara realized that Scarlett was offended with the last part. She placed her palm gently at the right arm of Scarlett and said, "I'm sorry...I shouldn't have said like that"

"That's alright. Many people hate me because I'm carefree but caring at the same time. It's normal"

"Christ No. I don't hate you. It was just a frustration"

"I understand. I'm just trying to help you. I came here because you asked me to"

"I'm so sorry. I'm such an idiot. I really am. You see, this is exactly why I can't get going in my life. I mess up everything, very easily"

"That's an awfully heavy statement. How about we

just pause for a second, take a deep breath each and start all over again?"

"Sounds great. Let's do it"

Both women gulped the remaining liquid from the respective glasses to the end, placed the glasses on the bar, closed their eyes and took deep breaths. When Tiara opened eyes, she saw Scarlett smiling, "So…" said Scarlett by placing her hands on her respective knees, "let's start again"

"I want to meet your boyfriend Damien"

"My boyfriend?"

"Damien. The one who wrote the book and tried to kill you. Don't tell me you've forgotten already. Is your life that good?"

"I wish", Scarlett giggled, "He never returned. He's gone from my life. I have no idea if he's even alive or not. Why do you want to meet him?"

"Because he wrote that book. He has a deep insight about bullies and some cool ideas, like starting a religion. Can you believe it? Starting a religion? Just to end bullying? Isn't the guy great? I'm sorry, he tried to kill you, but regardless, he's not normal. What do you think?"

"Absolutely. He… is not normal. But you are right in a way. He had some good ideas. I'll have to be really honest with you. I had worked hard for the book. I had helped him conceive some of his ideas about religion. I told him stories of people I know. All those stories that you read in the book, they're all about my friends. I sponsored the book. I made visits to agents and publishers. I worked much much harder", Scarlett paused for breathing, with her nostrils flared and eyes closed. Then she composed herself and said, "I can help you with everything you need. None of us need Damien. Consider him dead"

"Okay…", Tiara said pensively, "He's dead. From now on. But…how will you help me?"

"Let me start with the easiest step. How much do you know about bullying?"

"I know as in?"

"There are numerous resources over the internet, some of them are sponsored by government bodies, charity and non-profits organizations. Thousands of books, podcasts, videos, online groups and communities. You ask for help; people are there to help you. They are going to tell you exactly how to tackle your lack of confidence, self-belief or whatever you want to name it. Have you…ever tried any of those?"

Tiara had to admit that she did not try any of those earlier. She never read books. Reading any online content for more than five minutes made her drowsy.

She could manage with podcasts or audibles, but she was completely unaware of the resources so far.

For the next half hour and or even more Scarlett started showing her online contents, sending her invitations to Instagram communities, links to non-profit organizations and audio links. Tiara was overwhelmed with information. She was also embarrassed thinking how little she had known about a problem that the world had been trying to solve for more than thousands of years.

After her phone and mind were loaded with trillions of bytes of information, Scarlett paused and ordered another drink. Tiara had become fond of her already. She asked, "You seem to know so much about this. What have you been doing? How do you know all these?"

"I will...certainly...tell you my story another day. Like I said, I was a big helper while writing the Omni book. I've done enormous research; reached out to hundreds of volunteers, experts, psychologists and victims. You won't believe me, but I'm actively involved in a couple of non-profit organizations who have been trying to help bully victims and mental illness caused by that. I've met people who have suffered a lot. You're no different. I genuinely can help you if you trust me"

"Scarlett, I trust you more than anyone. I've never seen so much passion. Just tell me how. I'm with you"

"Erm…Here's the thing", Scarlett rubbed her face with her right palm, then adjusted her hair to the back and said, "I know a few people who had difficult times at different stages of their lives. Almost like yours or even worse. Some of their chronicles are written in the book like stories. You could read them at leisure. They had really really difficult times. But they survived and are doing quite well. I want you to meet them. Talk to them. Understand what they are going through and how they deal with it on daily basis"

"You mean like a rehab-rehab? Is there a concept like that for people like us?"

"A little more than rehab. You will see. These people are normal. They don't need any treatment. They have overcome their difficulties themselves"

"When can I meet them?"

"Guess it's your lucky day. We are having a small gathering at my place this Friday evening after work. I want you to show up"

"That's nice. That's really nice of you"

"See, it was easy. Helping is easier than bullying"

"Totally", Tiara smiled. Scarlett's warmth had won her heart completely. She wished Scarlett stayed a little longer and they spoke about their pasts, presents, favorite movies and everything under the sun, while the people in the pub moved in and out as if they did not exist, as if the pub was an endless maze, as if Tiara and Scarlett were lost in the maze with no particular hurry to find their way out.

"I got to visit a friend… in a hospital. Visiting hours will close soon. I should get going", Scarlett placed a credit card on the bar waiting for John.

"Hospital? Is everything alright?"

"He's been in a coma for the last few months. I visit him every week. Do you want to join me? He wouldn't know you are there. He doesn't even know I visit him", Scarlett smiled dry.

Stuttering for a moment, Tiara said, "I will. I will join you"

On the way to the hospital, Scarlett continued praising one of the organizations she was volunteering for. They counsel children who come to them for help. Scarlett had spoken to many victims who had a difficult childhood. Their stories were heartbreaking. She also told stories about traveling to faraway places like Colombia or Ethiopia or Bangladesh, out of her own interest, in the quest of searching how human beings at different parts of the world suffer from collective bullying day over day. It's the fate of the common people that interests her, not the people who went to war or to prisons.

Soon, the taxi reached the four storied building made of red old bricks. When they entered the building Tiara noticed that her regular company of light drizzle had already begun. Another gloomy evening was on the cards. Tiara was uncertain what she was going to see and was strongly longing to go back to her room for a solitary time, with red wine and the audios Scarlett had just sent.

Scarlett was familiar with the place. She was able to navigate quickly to the room in seconds. Many of the staff could recognize her easily and one of the nurses even spoke about her daughter's soccer game coming weekend. Scarlett was a popular person. She was lively and passionate enough to attract attention easily. Tiara felt like hiding herself in a shell if there was one around her.

An old man with white hair and crumpled skin, was lying on the bed with a complete setup of artificial breathing around him. It was evident that the man was in a coma, perhaps for many days. Nurses had done a remarkable job of maintaining his hair and beard. He looked trimmed, as if fresh from the bath but eyes closed. Scarlett bent near him and whispered something in his right ear while Tiara observed the room. It was a regular government hospital. Tiara had experiences of visiting hospitals many times with her mum on days when the staff were allowed to bring family along. She knew exactly how the hospital smelled. This was no different. Tiara observed Scarlett standing silently beside the bed for a couple of minutes. Slowly, Scarlett retreated and turned towards the door. Tiara followed. She was not comfortable standing near someone who was barely living.

"Do you want to tell me something?" Tiara asked Scarlett as they stepped out of the room.

"His name is Todd. He's the uncle of a friend of mine. He lived happily with his family and friends. Many people loved him. Many didn't. Like most of us, living an ordinary life"

Tiara decided to stay silent to let Scarlett speak.

"He had allergies from Mango, the fruit you know. You get them in bulk in the stores of East London. One day, at a party, someone gave him a dessert made of mangoes. He didn't know what he was eating. He finished a full bowl of it. Within minutes he started vomiting, right on the carpet where he was standing. His body bent and dropped on the ground. Everyone screamed to call the emergency. Someone said Benadryl was a quick cure and must rush for it. There was none at home. Meanwhile his body was shivering, eyes were rolling up and eventually…it started churning, like… as if he was being thrown inside a dryer. People tried holding him tight, but it went on for a minute. The emergency arrived exactly four minutes after his body became motionless. His eyes remained closed, but he continued breathing. They took him to the hospital. It was a terrible sight. I can never forget what I've seen"

Tiara placed her hand on Scarlett's shoulder. Scarlett wasn't crying. She was a strong woman.

"It was devastatingly hard on his family", Scarlett continued,

"They had been careful all along to keep him away from that fruit. All of a sudden, all efforts turned blank. His family deserved better"

"I understand. It wasn't your fault, right? You were just a bystander. You couldn't have done anything"

"Ever since that day, I visit him every week, hoping he has recovered. But there's no luck yet. I reckon I'll never be able to forget that traumatic experience. Sometimes I see his family here…they come more often, naturally. Some other friends do. He is unaware of everything"

"Strange things happen to people under strange circumstances. We are just helpless against such events. But you are doing a noble job Scarlett. You have compassion. My mum says, there's no such thing as compassion in the world. We live miserably without any real purpose. We are just like any animal. But you see, she's wrong. You're proving her wrong"

Scarlett smiled delightfully, "Where have you been Tiara? No one ever said so many good things about me on the same day"

"I'm not noticeable. Even if I was in your neighborhood, you wouldn't have noticed me"

10

The next few days unfolded rapidly. Tiara religiously listened to the podcasts, watched the videos and browsed every site that Scarlett had sent. They were helpful to some extent. People advised on how to control the mind, how to gain confidence and how to overcome different challenges at the workplace or any other difficult situations. Somehow, Tiara was not completely satisfied. She was looking for something with a personal touch. She thought she could visit one of those organizations next time with Scarlett. The idea of finding a volunteer job first and then converting into a full-time social worker, was fulfilling.

But at the same time, she could not stop thinking about Jacob's plan to get her the apprenticeship. Finding a story? What stories could she gather? How could she find something that was unique and relevant and never published before?

She had spoken to Jacob again. He provided tremendous encouragement, so much that Tiara started dreaming about her story published at the front page. Meanwhile, Scarlett was on chat with her, almost always. They chatted relentlessly, shared pictures, comments, live videos from Scarlett's work, Tiara's grocery shopping, Scarlett's gorgeous living room view, Tiara's tiny balcony, Tiara's morning run, Tiara's evening cooking, Scarlett's gym, Scarlett's bedroom and many more pictures from Scarlett's foreign trips. Energized with the newly found friendship, Tiara was hoping to utilize the Friday meeting into something meaningful; at least to learn more about the process. At the same time, she longed to meet Scarlett as soon as she could. Overall, she was looking forward to Friday.

On Friday evening, when Tiara arrived at Scarlett's building gate, she could recollect her first day of investigation. A strange satisfaction occupied her mind. She felt grateful that the investigation ever took place.

Scarlett opened the door with her usual smile. She was wearing a white full sleeve shirt and a black jeans. Her hair was tied at the back. As Tiara entered the living room, she noticed that two men and a woman were sitting at the dining table. All of them stood up to greet Tiara. Scarlett introduced them clockwise; a clean-shaven man at his middle age with full of black hair, as

Boris; a man with thin metal frame glasses and gelled blond hair with shades of gray in between, as Trent and finally the woman, who appeared at least ten years elder to Tiara, with black hair and a pair of tired eyes with dark patches around them, as Helen.

"Guess this is it", shrugged Scarlett, "Others won't be able to make it today. Help yourself Tiara, there are some freshly made cookies by Helen, and the tea beside. And I got coffee for you specially. I remember you like coffee"

Tiara was awestruck for a second. It was typical Scarlett; always planning ahead of everything. Tiara noticed at the center of the table a large plate of cookies was placed beside the pot of tea, pot of coffee, creme and sugar. Tiara served herself the coffee and added the creme to it. While stirring well with a spoon she glanced at the window, like the first time when she had entered this room. Glowing city lights had created enchanted impressions across the glass windows. Tiara could not turn her eyes away. She wondered, if someday, the city went into darkness, perhaps due to a power failure, what this room would look like.

Trent sipped from his cup, smiled at Tiara and said, "Tiara...a lovely name. I've never met a Tiara before. Tiara. How musical"

Tiara returned the smile, "That's very kind of you"

"I like it too. It's a very nice name", Boris spoke with a heavy Russian accent. It was quite a while Tiara had spoken to a Russian. She tried to recollect, when was it last time?

"A friend of Scarlett, are you?", Trent asked politely.

"Kind of. We came to know each other a couple of months ago", Tiara replied thoughtfully.

"I think we are more than kind of friends", Scarlett laughed out loud with index fingers of both hands indicating a quote around the word 'kind of'. Everyone joined the laughter. Tiara was wondering where this conversation was heading to. She looked at the windows again. The illuminated city looked stunning, more than ever before she had seen. As she looked up at the sky, she realized that the sky was squeaky clear; perhaps the silence before it imploded into a storm.

"You might have guessed already that Scarlett has told us briefly about you" Trent folded both his hands together while rubbing the tip of his two fingers from each hand together, "Scarlett also said that you would be benefitted by meeting us. As you can see, we're just ordinary people. This is not a rehab or a therapy session. So, tell me Tiara, do you have something in mind? Any expectations? What are you exactly looking for?"

Tiara adjusted herself for a moment on the chair. It was a comfortable chair to sit on. She noticed that she had dropped her handbag by the side of the large red chair where Scarlett was sitting on the first day. Tiara then said, "Well…I actually…don't have any idea. I don't even know what you guys are talking about. Scarlett said that all of you, at some point in time…have been through difficult times because someone…or a group of people were bullying you constantly. If I understood that correctly…you guys and I are on the same boat. Like Scarlett said, perhaps, you'll be able to tell me how to become normal again" She realized she was almost stuttering. Did she need those sandbags again?

"So you don't think you are normal?" asked Helen.

"In a way, I don't know what normal means. If it means someone making a successful life earning decent, living independently, receiving love and care and affection from people around, then yes, I'm not the one. I don't have any of those…"

Trent interrupted, "When I was bullied, I lost all my confidence over the years. I was just like you, unable to think clearly, unable to find something to hold on to. Then slowly, I started getting back to regular life. I didn't take help from any therapist or any motivational speaker or any online material. It was just me. I spent days thinking over what happened to me. Then one day, I realized that it was much easier than one could think.

I didn't have to look any further. The solution was right in front of me"

Tiara admired the way Trent had stopped beating around the bushes. With his commanding authority, he was certainly the leader of the group. Tiara imagined that the others must have been staring at him but looking around the table, she realized that the room had started to become darker. The ceiling lights were not switched on; but the solo standing light beside the bookshelf at the other side of the room, was on, creating a gloomy zone outside its reach.

Trent stood up from his chair and walked towards the window. Stretching his arms to the sides he said, looking outside the window, "Let me explain" He turned towards the table and looked at Tiara. Then he spoke in a clear but whispering voice that sounded like a dramatic narration from a thriller movie, "When you are bullied you lose your pride. You long for justice. Quite often, when you are desperate, you want to hit back. But the other side is stronger than you. You are not sure whether you could be effective at all. Therefore, you stay silent and the bully rolls on. This is the typical format of our lives. You see Helen there. She suffered for years. You would cry if you knew her story. And Boris, and Marcello, and Maggie, and many more of us. Next time let's hope we can all meet together. Each one of us here… has a story; a past; that does not let us sleep at night. It comes back haunting…when we are alone sleeping…in the form of a nightmare. Each one of us… went through depression, trauma; lost all confidence; can't trust anyone anymore. Ask yourself? You've gone through the same. People like us didn't receive any justice. No one helped us when we needed it. There was no support from friends or family. We were left alone to face the bully. Then one day, the bully moved on. They always do. They find new schools or colleges or jobs in new places. Years have passed, they live a normal life. They are married with children, living in large homes with cars and pets and backyards, drinking expensive wine, going to exotic vacations. Meanwhile, we…are in constant struggle. We have been reading inspirational books, listening to great voices speaking great stuff online, watching spiritual videos but nothing is helping. Some of us even visited psychiatrists regularly"

Trent's confident style had already casted a spell on Tiara. Barbara would have said, "He knows his onions". Trent continued before she said anything, "Do you know why nothing is helping?"

Tiara was silent. She shook her head from side to side. Glancing around the table she noticed that everyone was looking at Trent. Boris was moving his index finger rhythmically but very slowly on the table. Tiara wasn't sure what Boris was thinking.

"It's because..." Trent continued, "Everyone, including the psychiatrist is telling us that we need to be brave and composed and confident. We need to forget the past and try to move on. We need to look forward to brighter sides from the event by analyzing what we have learnt from it. Do you know what people like us do in America?"

Tiara remained quiet. She knew the answer.

"They become so depressed that they pickup guns and shoot innocent children in school. Media talks about American laws for the next few days. Some people suggest more spiritual methods to heal troubled individuals. They rue that faith is disappearing from society. But no one seems to know what the real remedy is. Killing innocent people is an act of terrorism. That can never cure a mind. What exactly can cure the mind of such people? It's us. We are the cure"

Tiara nodded her head in anticipation and said, "Right. I started reading the book Scarlett had given me. It talks about a religion which teaches kindness...well, every religion teaches kindness, but this one instructs on just one point. It says that never ever harm anyone. Is that the remedy you are talking about?"

Trent's whispering voice turned more melodious

and dramatic "I'm talking about something more. Something more direct"

Tiara blinked twice as she looked around again. Trent's gaze was quite unnerving, making her uncomfortable. She could not look into his eyes for a long time. There was something sinister which Tiara could not comprehend yet. The room had turned into complete silence. Scarlett had tilted her head backward looking at the ceiling. Boris and Helen were listening intensely. An electric heater, or something similar in the next room, was making a low hissing sound at regular intervals. Besides that, it was silent as a void. Tiara thought she would hear her own heartbeat. Trent was still standing in front of her with the halo from the city lights behind him. Tiara thought she had seen such postures before, in horror movies.

"So what are you?" Tiara asked apprehensively.

"We are bully hunters"

"Bully hunters?"

"Yes. Bully hunters. We hunt bullies"

"What…does that even mean? Hunting bullies…"

"We hunt them. The bullies. Those bullies who have long been forgotten by people and now living perfectly normal lives in different parts of the world. They never remembered us; because we were just one among many they crushed on their journey. Have you ever thought about what the person who bullied you…may be doing now? Were you ever curious to know?"

"Hmm…I've never thought about this. I'd say, I wanted to avoid that thought. I do know where she lives because my mum knows everything about everyone. Other than that, I don't, really don't, have any desire to know where she is"

"But we do. We want to know where they are. How they've been doing. Where they are working and so on"

"Why exactly would you do it?"

"Because the bully had enjoyed enough in his or her life. Now it's our time. It's the time they paid back the piece of happiness they had robbed from us"

"Are you saying…revenge?", Tiara gasped.

"If that's what you want to name it. Yes. Revenge. Revenge is the only remedy. If we see them suffering, writhing in pain, embracing depression…we'll feel that justice has been served. The only remedy to our sadness is to see them sad. The only remedy to our wound is to see them wounded. That's exactly what we do. We hunt bullies and inflict wounds on them. When we return home, we are satisfied. Our depression disappears. We become confident again. We can trust people again. In other words, we become normal again. Look at all of us here. We are all married, had children, they went to schools and colleges, we had regular jobs, friends, relations. But…none of that…was able to cure our problem until…we discovered the pleasure of bully hunting. Since then, there was no looking back. We are always helping each other and new friends of ours, like you"

Trent paused. Unable to believe what was going on, Tiara looked at Scarlett for rescue, but Scarlet was staring at the ceiling. Tiara wanted to leave. The hypnotic gaze of Trent was going to make her sick by the time the meeting ended.

Trent sat down on the same chair again and continued, "You may say, why is it such a big deal? Many people, literally thousands of people in our country, face bullies at some point, especially when they are young. And it's just our country. Let's not even count how many countries there are in the world. Most people just move on, accepting defeat…accommodating loss of many years or even decades in their journey. They'd tell their children that there are bullies at every stage of life and all we need…is to be strong and confident. Do you think that really works? Being strong? courageous? Maybe it does for some, but when circumstances are the worst, chips are down, even the most courageous person retreats. And most importantly, what about justice? Why will the bully who tormented me for years, live a comfortable happy life while I seek consolation in spirituality? Do you think that's justice?"

Tiara shook her head indicating she agreed with Trent. She was beginning to gather her thoughts back after the initial setback.

"The only way we can find solace is when we see them suffering. See their life being ruined"

"Schadenfreude!"

"There you go. You read the first chapter already. So, you're beginning to agree with me?"

"Well…", Tiara licked her lips. She was thirsty, "Someone said, an eye for an eye makes the whole world blind"

"Was it Martin Luther King?" asked Boris.

"Gandhi", Helen prompted.

"Right. Gandhi. Revenge is never the right solution…", Tiara looked at Trent.

"It's complete bollocks" Trent chuckled, "Gandhi calculated wrong. At the end of this eye for an eye battle, one person would remain with just one eye. Who do you think that person should be? The woman who bullied you? or yourself? The choice is yours. If we let her go, she'd bully someone else, then someone else again. We, humans, are genetically defective. You know how? Because we derive pleasure from others' misery. We love watching boxing where a man breaks another man's jaw. It's a pleasure. This type of pleasure sport has been popular since many centuries. People enjoyed watching gladiators...matadors. Why do you think they do so? Because that's how humans are. We want to see others' misery. That's the root of the bully. We, when we quote unquote hunt them, we are not defying any laws of nature. We'll derive pleasure from their pitiable situation. The bully has had her time. Now it's your turn to return the favor. Seize the day. Carpe Diem"

Gathering more strength, Tiara managed to say, "I don't know I should agree with you. This sounds like spreading violence in the name of justice. How can that be a noble step towards improving mankind?"

Trent scoffed, "It's not our job to improve anything in mankind or humankind, like they say nowadays. Where was humanity when we were suffering? You tell me, do you remember anyone standing by you when you had your worst days?"

Tiara shook her head agreeing with Trent.

"You know the answer. No one cared. So why... should we care? Forget humanity. Forget the conscience. Just follow the raw human brain that wants to see blood"

Tiara wished Scarlett ended the conversation. Her throat was now dry. She had to speak with more effort, "So how do you hunt these bullies?"

"Bully hunting is well organized. We as a group

meet regularly…discuss our pasts. Then we prepare a list of people we want to hunt. Then we assign each of us the responsibility of tracking a bully down. Boris, for instance, is tracking the bully of Paulo. I am tracking Maggie's. Jamal was tracking…"

Tiara interrupted, "Jamal? The guy who committed suicide?"

"You know him as well? That's impressive. Yes, him. Likewise, we share responsibilities"

"How do you track? How do you find out where that person lives?"

"It's much easier than you would think. Really it is. We start with simple steps like asking people in the old neighborhood, searching on Instagram, LinkedIn, Facebook, Snapchat and places like that. Everyone is vocal these days, everyone has opinions. Everyone is proud of sharing lovely pictures of their home and vacations. It's that easy. Then track down the address"

"How do you find time for this? I mean, all of you are working. It's not like me", Tiara tried to dilute the atmosphere, but no one appreciated the joke.

Trent continued in a slow voice that sounded like coming out of an old recorder playing in slow motion "We must find time. This is our life. We must bring justice to it"

Tiara maintained a straight face and asked "When you track them down. What do you do?"

"It depends. Really depends on what looks most suitable at that moment. This weekend, for instance, Boris is visiting one of them. Would you like to see for yourself how that works?"

Tiara looked at Boris, "Me? Seeing how that works?"

Boris nodded, "It's very simple. *I give* you my phone number. You call me on Sunday. We *go to* the guy's place. Talk to him. I do all the talking. You just watch us."

"What do you talk about? I mean, like, do you actually try to make him confess that he was a bad guy and it's time for retribution?"

"Almost like that. Maybe a little more. You will see. It's not something we can plan before. Really depends on the situation", as he spoke, Boris presented the phone screen displaying a number to Tiara to note down his phone number. Tiara diligently noted that down in her phone. She noticed almost two hours have passed since they met.

"So, Tiara, tell me, what do you think after everything we've told you?" Trent spoke again.

"I…" Tiara looked at Scarlett again who was now looking at Tiara, "I…don't have any opinion. It's way too much to take in. This bully hunting, revenge, pleasure from pain, I've never thought like that, ever. I'll take some time to digest them. But thank you, thank you for opening my eyes to a different direction"

"Pleasure was all ours Tiara", Trent nodded his head forward, "Is there any other question I can answer for you?"

"Well, I was just wondering…why Jamal?"

Before Trent replied Helen raised her right hand and said, "He wasn't really one of us. What he needed was some money and encouragement to stage his play. It was about a system of forced labor, back in the middle east. People from some poor countries went there to work. Their passports were seized and basic human rights. In a way, it's bullying, but on a much larger scale. We couldn't have done anything to solve the real problem. All we could do was to fund his work"

Tiara pointed her thumb to Helen.

"If you like what we do, you'll be one of us. Then we track down your bully. Trust me, that'll be the end of your miserable days and nights. You'll be able to live again"

Tiara nodded head from back to front a couple of times. Then she stood up and said, "I think I should be going now. I didn't realize that I've spent so much time already. There's someone waiting"

"I'm sorry Tiara. It was my fault", Scarlett stood up too, "I should've checked the clock. Would you like one of us to drop you somewhere?"

"That wouldn't be necessary Scarlett. Thank you for everything. I should be able to go by the tube"

"I think we should all be going. We have families waiting as well", Helen smiled. As everyone started walking towards the door, Tiara looked at Scarlett's eye but could not read what Scarlett was thinking. She looked at the windows one last time and felt claustrophobic. City was bright and staring at her. It was time she headed out.

A few minutes later, standing outside the building, she waited near the corner of the entrance. Once she was sure that two men and the woman were out of sight, she texted Scarlett, "I am waiting outside your building. We need to talk"

Within five minutes Scarlett came out of the building. She winked at Tiara, "You didn't give me a chance to change my dress. I had to rush after seeing your message"

"Let's take a walk down the bridge. We're going to walk until we finish talking"

"Oop-to-do. You are serious. Are you upset about this? Did I hurt you?"

"If I learnt anything from the Met job is not to jump into conclusion too soon. That's why I'm not drawing any conclusion on what I've just witnessed. I want to hear it from you. Let's talk"

11

The Pavements at both sides of the bridge were still crowded. People going back from work or from pubs or from somewhere else, were moving at their own casual pace, without any sign of any kind of rush. It was the beginning of the weekend. There was an air of relaxation among everyone. Traffic was ambling in the middle of the bridge. Tiara looked around the river. There were boats with bright lights on them, sailing lazily towards the east. Looking to the west, Tiara could see the glimpse of the illuminated London Eye and shining new tall buildings.

Walking brisk through the crowd, Scarlett said, "I'm not sure this is a good idea. This place is crowded. Why don't we go somewhere quiet?" Scarlett said after slowing down a little.

"It will be fine. I can hear you clearly", Tiara maintained her heavy tone.

"Right then. What do you want to know?"

"For a starter, tell me why…you are running a secret society?"

"Jesus Tiara", Scarlett stopped close to a signal board interrupting the flow of the crowd, who continued moving forward by dodging them, "It's not a secret society. We are meeting in secret, that's true. But, by no means, we are a secret society"

"Then what are you? You guys are…clearly working on a mission. You guys spoke about revenge, hurting other people. Are you guys criminals? You are trying to bring on more people, like me, to join you. What do you call it? Hey, a fun fact, not all people who meet in secret for a mission are secret societies, but they are just friends!" Tiara's voice reflected sarcasm.

Scarlett looked down. Then she looked away to the river. Tiara could see the boats and their lights and the numerous concrete structures huddling the river from both sides. Scarlett delicately asked, "Have I ever mentioned my mother to you?"

"Yes you did. During the investigation. You said she had died many years ago"

Scarlett took a deep breath and said, "Well, I lied. She left me, and my father. I can't tell whether she is alive or not, because I have no idea where she is. She never had any contact with us. Even if she did with my father, he wouldn't tell me"

"You lied to the police?"

"This information was not relevant to your investigation. How does it matter? She doesn't exist. I wish she was really dead"

Scarlett paused. Tiara walked a step closer to Scarlett and asked, "How old were you, when she…?"

"I was ten. I was big enough to understand everything. Until she left, our life was good. Our home was great, my school, our neighbors, friends; I remember everything. We lived in Hammersmith; in a gorgeous flat. My father would leave for work early in the morning and return home late at night. He wore different suites each day. His closet was full of stunning suits. I'd stand and count them. Some of them were smooth; I could still remember the touch," Scarlett paused.

"And your mum?"

"She stayed home. She played cello when she was young. I have seen the cello packed in our closet. I used to love its red color. Anyways, I don't remember anything else she was interested in. My mum was the most beautiful woman I have ever seen. She paid lots of attention to herself. She would spend time working out. I was wrong when I said…she was not interested in anything else. She liked to look beautiful. She spent on clothes…and makeup…and accessories. All expensive stuff. My dad loved her. I can't tell now…after so many years…whether she loved him too"

Scarlett started strolling again. Tiara joined at the left-hand side.

"I had no clue she was having an affair. I suppose she was hiding it well because she stayed home during most part of the day. The man was probably coming home. My father later told me he didn't have the slightest idea either. We would never know who the man was. The day she left, she had prepared my dinner and left a note on the fridge to remind me. She also had left a letter on the bed for my father. I never got to read the letter by myself. My father told me that mum had left with someone"

"Did he try to find her?"

"No. He was too devastated at first. Then…the police advised him that it was a conscious decision… not an abduction. So…he stayed home with me for a couple of days. We watched tele, ate popcorn and played video games together. Every time I missed my mum, my dad would start something new, like watching a new movie or start reading a book randomly. It worked for a short period, but a time came when he was supposed to return to work, and I had to return to school. He invited a few of his friends and my uncle and aunt from Harrow, to discuss the matter. I stayed inside my room that evening. I remember standing by the door, with my ears stuck to it, trying to hear my best to understand what the discussion was. I couldn't make anything out of it. Later, next day, my father told me that I'd be moving to uncle's house temporarily until he was able to control his situation better, my father would say, put my ducks in a row"

They reached the end of the bridge. Scarlett turned back and started strolling in the opposite direction. Tiara followed. Scarlett continued, "At first, I cried. Cried a lot. Then I was angry. I stopped talking to him. Then I threw my dinner away. But all in vain. My father was numb. He was neither listening nor thinking. I was familiar with my uncle's home, but it was a huge huge change for a child. The whole thing, especially those last few days, were imprinted in my memory forever. I don't quite understand how I survived that storm and why I survived"

"This uncle of yours, how was he related?", Tiara asked.

"He is my mum's own brother. Life at uncle's place was quite a struggle from the beginning. My aunt, for some reason, started to hate me. It could be because she hated my mum's affair and eloping. It could be something else, could be anything. I'll never know that. She made me realize that I was living there at her mercy.

The arrangement was that my father would pay a fat amount every month as my expense. In return, they're going to raise me like their own child. I started going to a new school, met new people, new routines, new rules. The whole world changed in front of my eyes. It was all because of my mother. She left me literally, on the road"

"Did your uncle...have own children?"

"They did. Two boys. We played occasionally together. They were quite nice to me. They treated me like their sister when their mother was not watching. She terrorized everyone in the home. My uncle would obey everything she had to say. Even when she was making me wash the dishes, he'd turn his eyes as if he was reading something. I had to work hard for a shelter"

"What was your father doing? When did he manage to take you back?"

"He never took me back. He visited me every weekend at the beginning. I cried near him about everything that was happening. He consoled me saying that life had been hard on everyone at the same time, and everything would be alright very soon. A few months later...I started seeing him less frequently. Sometimes, only once a month. One day, my uncle mentioned that he had been traveling to America very often and he was seriously considering a move there. That gave me new hope. A lot of hope indeed. But guess what, my father told me that it would be the best arrangement for everyone if I stayed back. By that time, I had already started losing certain emotions. I remember I did not cry. After he left, I went back to my dark days and...darker nights. My aunt continued dominating every aspect of my life, my father continued sending money and myself, the golden goose of my aunt, lived miserably"

"I have to say, your story is very similar to fairy tales, or fantasies. I don't read books normally, but I've seen all the parts of Harry Potter and read Cinderella when I was little. You just blended the two in one story and are trying to sell me as your story. Clever one, Scarlett", Tiara stopped around the same place where they had halted earlier.

Scarlett sighed. Placing her elbows on the railing, she bent forward; with her eyes disturbed and hair billowing to the sides of her face, she was lost in thoughts. Tiara bent forward on the railing as well.

"You don't believe me, do you?", Scarlett said while looking away.

"No, because it's not even possible in our country. Anyone, in your place, would dial the child abuse reporting line. And you're telling me you didn't do that?"

"I didn't. Believe it or not. I didn't have the courage. My aunt was extremely clever. She had already threatened me that reporting anything to the police or teacher or anyone else would cause severe consequences to my life. Police would involve my father who would again hand me back to my aunt. I believed her, until I realized I was stupid. But it was too late already"

"Okay okay. Let's say for fuck's sake, I believe you, even though you lied to me and police at convenience, say I believe you. What happened next?"

"Can't you see what happened? Myself...Scarlett... happened. Remember, when you met me in the pub, you said how much you had struggled against bullies in your entire life, how... your life... had changed, and you became depressed and all other stuff? Mine is no different. Your bully was in your neighborhood. Mine was inside the same four walls. My aunt shaped the rest of my childhood. I was terrified all the time, lacked confidence at every step, slept less, had no toys, worked at home, played very little, couldn't trust or like other kids in school...and what more? Take a guess, I could manage really really poor results at school. Those eight years were the decider of everything I was going to do next. They shaped me; into a miserable, failed, depressed and mediocre woman"

"Again, what was your father doing?"

"Like I said, he was in America. He would speak to me over the phone. When I was angry, I wouldn't speak even that. He continued sending money. As I was growing up...I realized that I wasn't able to trust any friends in school...I know I keep saying that... but that's how I was... I could hang out with them but there was no strong bond. At home, aunt continued her dominance, but I was getting battle hardened. One thing was clear to me that I had to run away from my aunt. With my result, I had very few chances to make it to anything good. When I was accepted to a faraway uni in the north, I was ready to go...by all means. My aunt tried to bully me again...but she realized that I was desperate and could go to any extent to get my freedom. But then...life at the uni presented a different challenge. My confidence was low, attention was very little. I started performing poorly again. I was living in a small flat with two other girls. They were smarter, had ambitions...I tried to be normal as much possible but let me tell you...at times...when I'm alone at home, especially late nights, something, would press me from all around...I can't explain in words what that is...it's a force, a void, that would surround me like a thick blanket, start to choke me from within...everything in my life would appear meaningless, I'd pity myself, or hate myself so much that...at times, I felt...I must end all misery. I couldn't stand those girls much longer. I realized that I was going to be suicidal very soon. Everyone around, absolutely everyone, appeared successful and happy to me. At every step insecurity crippled me. My internal monologue continued telling me that I was useless. A fear of defeat controlled my senses. I started staying high most nights, skipped classes during days sleeping, then spent the next night in horrible conditions again. I had no close friends because I couldn't trust anyone. I was hanging out with people…as long as there was alcohol flowing. I was… I was just waiting for my graduation to complete. One day, I spoke to my father, asking if I could leave the uni, go back to London for some work. That would probably keep me busier. I also wanted to see a therapist…but…most of all…I desperately wanted to go back. For some strange reason, that evening, my father sensed the urgency in my voice and agreed. He flew over from New York, took me to London where we stayed in a hotel for a week. We shopped for a flat where I'd be moving in after I finished my college. I was grateful to him, at least that one time, for giving me some financial freedom. He arranged lots of finances around me… those things made my life very comfortable. He had told me that he was making a real envious amount of money and my comfort was his topmost priority. When he said that, I made him swear on me that he was not in love with anyone else. Sometimes, he is pretty sweet. You know…" Scarlett paused to breathe.

They started walking again. There were much less people on the sidewalks now. Scarlett continued,

"So, that was my story. How I lost my precious childhood. How I was bullied. How I became a nobody. Sometimes, I used to think, why me? Why did my mother have to leave? Why did my father not have better plans for me? But I'm helpless. I had no control over events"

Tiara continued walking silently. She was thinking of Scarlett's story.

"Are you going to say something?" Scarlett asked.

"Scarlett...I...I feel sorry for you. I didn't know any of these. I always thought you are a happy go lucky person"

"It's alright. Not your fault. Most often we don't recognize a depressed person at the first sight. Look at yourself. You had a bad life, as bad as me. But you know what the worst part is? When the bully is at home. You could at least hide safely inside your home but for me, the home was the war zone. I hated every moment of my stay over there. I still hate my aunt. I've never met her again since I moved out of their home. I never reached out where they were...never picked up their phone calls or replied to their messages"

"How about them? Did they try to contact you?"

"They did. My uncle had called many times, but I

never answered", Scarlett sniffled, "And I'm not crying. I'm just extremely mad", with the back of her right palm she circled around her right eye and pointed to Tiara, "Do you see any teardrops? There won't be any. I don't cry over my past anymore because I've shed enough tears"

Tiara touched Scarlett's forearm affectionately and said, "I understand. I felt the same way. Maybe it's time I pressed my mum for an answer to what happened to my dad"

"You definitely should. There ought to be a secret behind his disappearance. But before we talk more, I'm kind of starving. I haven't touched any of those cookies. Should we grab something first?"

Tiara nodded, "Why not? We've been walking for a long time. Let's chill out a little"

12

They walked towards the north of the bridge for a while until Scarlett liked an Indian fast-food joint. She was delighted with the idea of chicken rolls. The place was crowded with people standing in a queue that reached the next shop's entrance, but the two women were perfectly happy to wait for their turn. The queue moved slowly while they resumed their conversation. Tiara cleared her throat and asked, "How did you manage to come out of the depression? I mean what you are now is a reasonably normal person"

"You think so?" Scarlett smirked by lifting her right corner of the lips upwards, "I still don't know myself...when I'm normal or when I'm crazy. Anyhow, flashback...flashback...after I moved to London I had absolutely no direction to life. My father was insisting that I must get back to higher studies, but I had no energy or motivation. I just wanted to get busy working.

He even took me to his home in Brooklyn. He lived alone; he didn't lie to me. His life was busy...from early morning to late night. While he continued working, I traveled a bit in the US, like most people do. My father thought travel could help me. He encouraged me to travel all around the world and I followed his advice. Someday, I'll show you the photos that I had taken from all the places I visited. Every year, you know, I go to a place, usually something far away, I read about it, know the people living there, their culture, their behavior... and...you know, the most important thing, I try to find people like me, who have been subjected to severe bullies and had no outlets to express themselves. I'd find agencies that helped bully victims, talk to the victims, try to know their stories...it's strange, you know! There are so many people suffering and I'm not even talking about any war or crime or systematic oppression. I only look for common people, their ordinary lives, and their misery. I'm going to take you along next time wherever I go"

Tiara sighed, "Lucky you. At least you have a great way to escape your pain. Some people, like me, can't afford such luxury. We are left behind to grind through our banal battle every day"

"Don't say that Tiara. Every depressed person has a story behind. Only the depressed person knows the burden of the story. I did go to a therapist. It was my father who had insisted all the way. I couldn't continue. Someone warned me and I then thought about it. I thought I'd be tied to those meds for the rest of my life. And it really happens. People get stuck for lives…if you remove their meds, they go insane"

"But what's the alternative? Not everyone can travel, read, relax like you did"

"We need to find what we want at that point in time. In my case, I wanted to work but something very light, just enough to meet my monthly needs of food and drink. What I really wanted was to know people. As many as I can. It kept me busy…"

The queue had moved to the counter, where they had to place the order. The man with a large mustache at the counter handed them a token which had seat numbers written on it. They found the seat at the corner of the room where the walls were decorated with Indian movie posters. Music that matched the atmosphere was being played from the speakers. The table had a jug of water and two glasses. After sitting, Tiara felt like she had been standing for many hours.

"So, you were talking about meeting people…" Tiara didn't want to lose the thread.

"I dated. A lot. I mean a real lot. Men, women…

as they came. All I wanted was to know them and find people who were like me"

"How would you do that?"

"I spoke to my dates for hours and hours. Learnt about them. Some were introverts…it's easy to tell who's going to open up and who's not…at the very first hour of conversation. Some were overly expressive. They liked to tell their stories. If I found someone who suffered so much like me, I'd connect to them again. And again. Then we'd become friends…discuss our stories. What I told you today, must have been discussed a hundred times so far", Scarlett laughed out. Tiara smiled.

"And that's how you built your secret society?" Tiara asked carefully.

Scarlett lifted her index finger and shook her head slowly, "Did you see us walking around a round table wearing a mask and nothing else, chanting a bizarre song?"

Tiara laughed out, "But you have a tattoo with a red flower in a black background. You also have the same paint on your nails. Isn't that a symbol of a society?"

"Oh my…you are creepy. How did you notice all that?"

"I just did," Tiara smiled.

"I liked the design of the tattoo that I did some years ago. So I thought of making a nail paint out of it. There's nothing special about the color or the flower. We're not a secret society. We're friends. At first, I met Trent from a date. It was a few years ago. Still, he was way way older than me but, I didn't care at all"

"Can I tell you something? I find Trent…kinda wicked"

Scarlett giggled, "He is indeed. Isn't he?"

"Isn't he married as well? I thought he said that"

"Like I said, people have their stories to tell for every action in their lives. I don't judge anyone. I wasn't looking for a boyfriend in him or in anyone else. That would be the last thing. I was looking for a person… who was like me. You've seen how passionate I'm about all this stuff. He was exactly like me, or even more… when I first met him…there was a fire in him…a sense of revenge was driving him. He told me that he wanted to go after the bullies. Not just his own but anyone who needed help"

"Like a superhero? Avengers?"

"Almost. He was ready to even visit my uncle when he heard my story. Soon we became friends. He introduced me to Boris. Meanwhile I was meeting…"

"And mating", Tiara giggled.

Scarlett laughed, "That too. many people. Our circle started growing bigger and bigger. It was like a chain, friend of friend of friend. I don't remember who brought Helen. She had suffered a lot. Poor thing"

"What did she suffer from?"

"Her son was horribly injured by a group of bullies from his school. They had a late-night party at someone's home. The boys were drinking. That night Helen received a call from the owner of the home that her son had fallen down from the terrace. He was hospitalized immediately. When he gained his consciousness, he could not move his face or hand or legs. A complete paralysis. It took them a very long time to bring him back to a manageable condition. He lost his school years, never graduated, never went to college. Helen and her husband had got him many support systems like full time care at home, special education but you see, a life was just destroyed overnight, and no one was held accountable"

Tiara was holding her mouth with both her hands while listening to it. Finally, she managed to speak, "How come? How come no one investigated what happened?"

"Boys were drunk. There were three older boys who were already known bullies. They had been bullying Ethan, Helen's son, for quite some time. Helen realized that it was them who pushed him but...the boys were united with their alibis. They spoke in unison that Ethan slipped while drinking. Much later...when Ethan was able to express his emotions…he conveyed to Helen about what had happened that night. But the case is too weak to be proven. No one saw the boys pushing Ethan that night"

Tiara's heart was aching for Helen. She couldn't collect any words. At last, she managed to say, "You guys are planning to attack that bunch of boys?"

"They are not boys, never have been. They are…a bunch of scamps, criminals. We're going to hunt them down. That day is not too far away"

The rolls arrived. Both women were hungry enough to silently eat them within five minutes. Once billing was settled, they were out again, aimlessly ambling towards the west side by the river, under the clear sky and occasional breeze that smelled Spring. Tiara remembered how she loved walking on crowded streets when she was young, in Stella's neighborhood. When she was in the ocean of people, no one noticed her, let alone trying to bully her. Even a walk in the high street at the busy evening hour, without any purpose or direction, used to magically heal her mind. She was feeling exactly the same, walking beside Scarlett. Tonight, was one of those moments, where all tireless people on the road were woven into their respective stories, so much that they did not pay any attention to someone like Tiara wandering in the midst.

Looking at Scarlett, who was walking with her head down, Tiara asked,

"Tell me about Damien. How did you meet him? By dating as well?"'

Scarlett looked into Tiara's eyes, as much as they were seen at night, "Have you read the book I gave you?"

"I tried. But as I have told you…"

"Yes you did. You don't like reading"

"But…when I was investigating your case, I visited the publisher of the book. They told me that you had worked very hard to publish the book. You loved Damien a lot, didn't you?"

"I worked hard to publish it, because…only because…I was the one who wrote it"

"Really? and you credited Damien for it?"

"I wanted to write a book about gathering my thoughts and ideas. Also, Trent had been thinking about the new religion thing. There are already two hundred thousand religions in the world. He said another one would anyway go unnoticed but still, we should document our effort, to warn ordinary people not to mess with others. When I wanted to publish the book, my father said something interesting that caught my attention. He said that men, in general, don't like to read novels written by women...unless of course it's something absolutely famous. However, they don't mind reading any non-fiction written by any subject matter expert. So a woman writer has only two options. If she wants to write a novel… the audience will be only women. Alternatively, a woman could write on a subject of her expertise. On the contrary, being a male writer, creates more options. There are still chances that men and even women would read a book written by a completely random man. So, after thinking on his suggestion, we decided to use a man's name", Scarlett paused.

"And Damien was okay with that idea?"

"You don't get it…read my lips"

After a brief pause, Tiara, agape, exclaimed, "It's your pen name!"

Scarlett smiled dry with anticipated rage from Tiara.

"My god. It was a complete lie! Jesus Christ Scarlett. How? and why?"

"Don't get mad at me please. There were reasons…"

"You keep lying. You lied all along. The whole case, oh my god…", Tiara frowned.

"Tiara, calm down"

Tiara walked towards the river and Scarlett followed. Tiara was breathing heavily.

"Are you alright?", Scarlett asked apprehensively.

"I'm okay. I'm okay…you…I just can't understand you"

"I am sorry. Really, I am. I told so many lies. It's only

because I had other plans. I had no idea I'd meet you among all these"

"I wish I had not met you"

Scarlett shrugged and said, "I was guilty...of something...more than one thing actually. That was one of the reasons as well why I wanted to publish the book. I wrote down some confessions in the book to offload some guilt. But the book...failed miserably. As my friends predicted, no one noticed it. My guilt was rising to the peak. And soon, those dark nights were back. I was forlorn in my apartment. The view from my glass windows...was like...as if the unforgiving maze of concrete all around...were trying to swallow me alive. I couldn't take it anymore. I spent time walking in my room...late at night... two or three days in a row because I just could not sleep. I was so vulnerable that I decided to end my life"

"What? You wanted to kill yourself?"

"When I hit rock bottom of my depression, that usually becomes the next thought. I thought I'd meet the people...who I think were my friends...for one last time. So, I hosted them over thinking that would be the last night of my life"

"And?", Tiara's eyes were about to pop out. She tried reading Scarlett's face. It showed determination.

"We partied late and had some fun...as much fun

as people like us could have. After they left, I tried gathering my courage to finish the due, but I could not. I was weak. We see suicides and murders in movies and books so often but when you try them on yourself, they are fucking difficult. I still remember that night in every tiny detail. It was a horror night for me. I could neither sleep, nor sit alone in the living room. The view from the window…like I keep saying, was a living monster wearing shiny armor. I was terrified even sitting, let alone kill myself. Close to the morning, I woke up from a quick nap, and gathered one final force of courage to hurt myself with that knife. Let me tell you, it was painful…an awful lot of pain. I realized that I just didn't have the guts. A person like me, has days…and nights…to think about unnecessary stuff. It wasn't surprising that I already had a plan B for a situation…when I failed to kill myself. The plan was to bring my story to the public. I could create a domestic violence scene which could force police to find Damien. I'd guide the police to the address where my friend lived and then the police would uncover everything…all my lies…and then, it would be instant newspaper gossip that an insane woman did some insane act to come to the limelight…and at least, then my book and my idea would be famous…people would read it…they'd know what I was trying to say…about bullying and the consequences…It would be a pebble in the pond… everywhere, in news and in social media. People would express their opinions and counter opinions. And who knows, one day…even the government would act on it, make bullying an act of crime. If not, at least, the bullies all around the world…would think twice before committing any act. They'd know that a group of people…are going to come after them. Even if it takes a decade or more, they'll be hunted down, for sure"

Tiara, rolling her eyes, exclaimed, "Incredible. You are incredible. You planned all these. You are…I don't know what to say. Did I just ruin your plan? Did you expect an experienced cop to expose the plot right away?"

"You didn't ruin anything. My plan was to bring it to the public but at the same time it had its own risks. If Anyone decoded the book, or my life, or my group of friends, anything could have happened. Who knows, we could have gone to jail"

"Then how did your friends allow you to publish the book?"

"They didn't believe anyone was going to notice it. I continued convincing them how guilty I was feeling about a couple of things. They were okay with the book to pacify my guilt. But they had no idea about my plan B", Scarlett grinned.

"What were you guilty of?"

"I told you to read my book", Scarlett smiled mysteriously. She then leaned by the railing to look deep into the dark water.

"That fucking book. You know what, I'm sorry, I was working at the Met that time and they sent me, instead of an experienced constable. It was all my fault that I couldn't make you famous"

"It's not that way Tiara. When I met you, I realized that you were one of us"

"Really?"

"I am serious. I noticed…on the very first day…just for a moment…a flash of profound sorrow in your eyes"

"You're making it up…"

"No I'm not. Why would I?"

"Because…I had the same feeling…just for a moment…I saw the same in your eyes"

"No way…"

"I swear. What are you, Scarlett? My reflection?", Tiara giggled.

Scarlett laughed, "Maybe I am. Who knows? Have you ever thought about why I withdrew the case?"

"I thought you were afraid of getting busted of something big"

"I wanted to befriend you. Look, I met so many such people in life, it hardly takes me any time to understand that you had a painful story too. That's why I dropped my plan B. I could do it another time, provided I was sad and guilty enough…and had long sleepless nights alone"

They started walking again, silently, both gathering thoughts or memories that could have been awakened by the beautiful night, breeze, river and stories.

"How did you decide on the name Damien?", Tiara finally broke the silence.

"My father had a colleague named Damien. He talked about the guy occasionally"

"And the picture?"

"I have no idea who that is. I just found it on the internet"

Tiara laughed out. Scarlett's eyes were glowing with amusement.

"And South Africa?"

"Part of my imagination. I loved the beauty of Cape Town when I visited. It was jaw dropping. Didn't take me much time to decide where my imaginary boyfriend came from"

"But you even told his year of immigration, like a genuine person"

"You have a very strong memory. Have you ever realized that? You should do something that needs memory"

"I wanna be a journalist, I've been trying to get a break there. I don't know...", Tiara looked down.

"That's great news. You're going to make it. I'm telling you. And coming back to immigration, yes, all my imagination"

Scarlett walked a few steps forward and twirled around with her arms stretched; her face, content and cheerful, her body resonating the vibe; making her look like a small child delighted with little joy.

"You know what, although I've spoken about my life hundreds of times, I've never felt so good. You are a wise listener. Thank you so much for listening today", Scarlett pulled Tiara's right hand slightly to indicate her gratitude. Tiara returned an affectionate smile and said, "I've been listening to my mum for the entire life. She created the great listener in me"

Scarlett twirled on her feet again. Then looking around the people she giggled, this time out of embarrassment. She was perhaps attracting attention.

"Just one last thing, before we finish your story", Tiara uttered.

"Anything...anything you ask", Scarlett was walking with little hops making it difficult for Tiara to match the strides.

"You told me, you were guilty. Why were you guilty and I want to hear from you, not from the book"

Scarlett stopped. Looking around and again carefully, she took Tiara's hand in her and started walking towards the edge of the water.

"What happened?", Tiara asked.

"We need some space".

When they found a relatively empty part, Scarlett stopped. Then she said,

"Today, in the meeting, Trent was trying to explain to you...things like hunting bullies and talking to them. Wasn't he?"

"Yes he was"

"Flashback, flashback...as we started making new friends, our group size was growing. Eventually, we started our operations. We'd discuss our lives first, then identify our bullies, not every one of them, but only the ones who shaped our lives to their current forms. Then, we plan to find them. Like Trent was telling you today. That's exactly what it is. We hunt the bullies. The forgotten bullies. Each one of us would be assigned to one bully. After we find them, we study them very well. Their strengths and weaknesses. Then we plan on confronting them. One at a time."

Tiara, expecting something like this, asked, "Yes. I got that already from the meeting. How do you confront them?"

"We would meet them. At home, or restaurant,

hotel whatever suits the plan. We explain to them how terrible their actions in the past have been. Sometimes, we demand apology, sometimes, compensation"

"In what form? What if they disagree? Do you hurt them?", Tiara's eyes were not blinking. She realized that she was breathless as well.

That momentary childishness had already disappeared from Scarlett's face. It was now straight and determined again. Her eyes showed nothing less than rage. She uttered slowly, "If the situation demands"

"Oh my god. Scarlett, what are you guys? Please tell me that you are messing with me"

"I am not Tiara. Tomorrow, when you join Boris for his mission, you are going to witness it. Boris is one of our finest. He'll be able to tell you a lot more. Answer all your questions."

"Jesus Christ Scarlett. Please tell me, please, you didn't kill anyone. Have you killed anyone?" The last few words were almost whispers. Tiara scanned around. There was no one beside the river water making its relentless small waves.

"I was guilty because someone, a bully, was injured, to the extent that he still hasn't recovered. I was there in front of him, when it happened, watching with pleasure, with anticipation that his body would writhe in agony, his mind would beg for mercy. It went a bit extreme. He couldn't recover from the attack. It wasn't a death but probably worse", Scarlett sniffed and closed her eyes.

Tiara's, breathless already, covered her mouth with both hands and then whispered, "That old man, in the hospital. It was him. Oh my god. Oh my god…"

"Calm down Tiara. He is alive. Doctor said he is going to wake up someday. I said, I am sorry …and… guilty as hell. You've seen me visiting him. I pay my tribute regularly. It wasn't my fault Tiara. I did not add the allergic food. It was…"

Before Scarlett could finish Tiara swung her right arm and landed a slap at the middle of her left cheek. With the sudden impact Scarlett lost her balance and fell on her knees to the ground. Holding her cheek she cried, "It hurts Tiara…"

Tiara cried loud, "You are a liar. Fucking serial liar. How can I trust you? Everything you said could be a lie. You harmed people. You are a criminal. You…just fuck off", She walked with fast steps towards the road while Scarlett sat down on her knees with her both hands holding her knees, head down. Without turning back, Tiara continued walking and managed to call a taxi. Soon Tiara was sitting in the taxi that headed towards east while some bystanders were surrounding Scarlett who was still sitting motionless on the ground. As the taxi moved forward by dribbling through Friday night traffic, Tiara started to feel incomplete. It was almost a perfect night. She was with a great company; someone she had been enjoying talking to since the last few weeks, someone who respected her, understood her emotions and perhaps, liked her too. She recalled her principle since the training days. Her failure to follow them had now cost her a special friend. She had jumped into the conclusion too soon. It was all too impulsive.

Sitting in the cab, staring at the streetlights that reflected in different shapes on the glass window, she convinced herself that she had just made a really huge mistake. Quickly taking her phone out of her handbag, she dialed Scarlett.

Scarlett picked up just after two rings.

"What do you want?" Her voice was dry, as if she had been coughing all along.

Tiara felt that a ball of emotion was trying to push out of her throat. She tried to swallow it first and then said, "Where are you now?"

"I am where you had left me"

"Stay there. I'm coming"

The taxi turned backwards by making its way through lanes and alleys as Tiara was hurrying the driver. When the taxi arrived, Tiara jumped out of it. She paid the driver quickly and ran towards the spot. Her handbag swiveled on her forearm, her hair swung by her shoulder and her heels squeaked with the contact of the cobblestones, as people around looked with amusement.

Scarlett was standing at the same place. Her hair was undone, mouth was swollen, and eyes were moist. It was the child again in her, who was looking for a shelter from a storm. When Tiara reached near her, she opened her mouth and murmured, "Don't you ever, ever, leave me like that again"

13

Tiara was able to see a large scissor that was cutting someone's hair. Both the person cutting the hair and the person sitting were wearing back gowns covering till their knees. Tiara had to walk inside the salon to have a clear view. There was a yellow bulb radiating from the ceiling and a large bright spotlight right beside the mirror. Going closer, Tiara could find an angle to see the reflection in the mirror. It was Trent sitting on the chair, with eyes closed, head already half shaved, and he was snoring. Looking upwards Tiara could see the face of the barber. Her body shivered; stomach twisted with ache. It was Stella in the mirror. Her eyes were pink; a part of her face was covered with her curls dropping sideways. Before Tiara could say anything, Stella moved the scissor swiftly to jam inside Trent's throat. A fountain of blood started spilling over. Trent screamed loud in agony. Tiara started choking as if there was no air in the room. Then she coughed a few times while trying to open her mouth.

A muffled sound came out of her dry mouth, and she opened her eyes. She felt her body had turned wet with excessive sweat. Looking around her bed, she realized that It was her familiar bedroom. Nothing had changed since she was last awake. To overcome the horrifying nightmare, Tiara tried sitting up on the bed by supporting her body on elbows. The back of her head responded with sudden ache and then the entire head felt heavy as if a gigantic rock was resting on it. She dropped her head on the pillow again and closed eyes. Lying there, with both hands holding her head tight, she tried to think how she had arrived here. She didn't know what time in the morning it was, but clearly there was a flood of sunlight in the room, indicating it could be way past morning. She must have been sleeping for a very long time.

She tried remembering how the night had progressed. Both the women agreed to have some drinks together and have some fun. Tiara recalled the first one was a Caprioska. They were hopping pubs. Scarlett was ecstatic, screaming like a child. They were dancing at some point, among a dense crowd under flashing red, green and blue lights. There were shots flowing all over. The next thing Tiara could recall was a black cab driver who was annoyed with Scarlett as she continued explaining the route to Tiara's place. There was no memory after that.

Slowly, Tiara opened her eyes again. She desperately needed to gulp some water. Still holding her head, she moved her body slowly up, then sideways to eventually pull herself out of the bed. She noticed that she was wearing the same clothes as last night. But the top now had large yellow marks at the front. What were they? Did she throw up badly?

Tiara walked slowly towards the medicine cupboard and was able to gather herself to take two paracetamols. She had to walk towards the kitchen for a glass of water. Pouring the water inside her throat, along with the tablets, Tiara realized that she was starving. There were some cookies on a newly purchased cookie box on the counter. Must have been part of Barbara's weekly grocery shopping. After eating two cookies she remembered that today was Barbara's day off. She had mentioned that sometime this week.

Almost limping, like a wounded animal, she reached Barbara's bedroom. The door was left ajar. She was probably watching television inside. Tiara just walked in. Barbara was sitting on the bed with her phone. Tiara could not comprehend she was reading news or social media or simply resting her eyes.

Tiara jumped on the bed and rested beside Barbara.

Without looking at her Barbara said in a sharp voice, "Don't come here without cleaning up your mess"

Tiara, tired of any conversation, asked, "What mess mum?"

"Ah…you don't remember. Jesus Christ. You are now going back in time. Do you think your age is reducing? Why are you behaving like a young girl?"

"What did I do? It's a terrible hangover mum. I don't understand what you are saying"

"You see. You have a hangover as well. I can't help you. I don't think anyone can help you. Where were you last night? Do you even remember that?"

"I do mum. I was with Scarlett"

"Who's Scarlett? Never heard that name from you before. Did you just make it up?"

"No. For god's sake. She's a friend. We were drinking a lot", Tiara pulled the pillow behind her head and stretched her body forward. It was a comfortable position.

"You drank so much that you don't remember that you threw up all over your bathroom floor. Not even in the toilet but on the floor. Look at your top. It's dirty. I am telling you. This is not acceptable. You still have no responsibility. You are drinking like a seventeen year old girl. When are you going to settle down? Have a stable job? I am not even asking anything else. Just learn to grow up Tiara. I am becoming tired of you", Barbara focused back on the phone. Tiara, with a deep sigh, closed her eyes again. It was pointless most of the time to argue with Barbara. All her conversation these days ended up complaining about Tiara's lack of responsibility.

"I am very happy, mum. I don't need anything morc", Tiara announced with eyes closed.

"Yes you do. You are a loner. There is no one around you. Everyone needs company. A partner, if not a family. I want to see you as a normal Tiara"

"What do you mean normal?"

"I didn't mean that you are not normal. I just meant I can't look at your loneliness. It hurts me. A couple of months ago, I saw you walking home, from the window that overlooked the street. You know what I saw? It was a foggy evening. I saw the body of yours walking through the fog. It was symbolic. You were all alone, in the mist. I cried that night. Tiara, I want you to do something with your life"

"I'm working on it...mum", Tiara's eyes were still closed. She had heard this conversation before a handful of times. It was not bothering her much. She continued with holding her right thumb and index finger together, "I...am...this close to starting my first story for a newspaper. If they get impressed, I might land a probational job there. Jacob promised he'll do everything to get me in"

"Do you trust his ability?"

"I do. This is the only thing I have. If I don't make this, I promise I shall think about going back to school. I've been starting to think that I need…some kind of degree…to start any job…there's too much competition out there"

"This is why you should have worked hard when you were young. Didn't I tell you? We make our way up with education. That's been the case for decades in our community. You couldn't have been different. But…not everything works as we want them to", Barbara sighed. She was still moving her fingers on the phone. Tiara glanced at her quickly to understand her real mood. Was she really worried or was it a usual bantering moment?

"Mum, I've been…uh…thinking a lot about this. I think I have the right to know what happened to my father. You've always been hiding the truth from me very cleverly. I really want to know the truth. I can't bear it anymore", Tiara uttered the words with care, hoping it would influence Barbara.

Barbara looked away from her phone to the window and said, "Is this a new tantrum of yours or is it because you are hungover, you are getting strange thoughts?"

"I am serious, mum. You need to tell me what happened to my dad"

"I had told you before. He left me after I conceived you"

"I know that you told me. But what happened after that?"

"I told you that too. I never tried to contact him. He was a rogue. It was a night's stand between us. He had no intention to move on with anything"

"And you chose to continue with the baby. Why so?"

"It couldn't have been my decision or your grandparents. It was God's will. His decisions are always correct and final for me. What happened to me was already decided by God. There was nothing much I could have done"

"I give up on you", Tiara got up from the bed. The headache was subsiding. She needed to see what she had done to the bathroom. While closing the door, she looked back, and asked, "What was his name again? You tell me different names at different times. Tell me the truth"

"I think…it was Garry. Garry…I can't remember the last name. It was so many years ago. I think… it started with the letter L", Barbara replied, still staring at the phone.

"Genius. If you ever remember, tell me the full name. I shall find him", Tiara moved towards the kitchen.

"How will you find him?", Barbara raised her voice from the room.

"I have my sources", Tiara went towards the bathroom door. The floor was messed up badly and looking at that, Tiara started feeling ashamed of her behavior. Going to her bed, she found her phone right under the pillow. It showed a missed call from Scarlett. She called back. Scarlett picked up just after two rings, "You alright Tiara?", Scarlett's voice was silky smooth.

"I'm okay. Just a bad hangover?"

"Good you are okay. I was worried. You're really in bad shape. I wasn't sure you would be able to reach home alone."

"It's not that bad though. I remember you got the cab for me. How did you reach home?"

"Took a cab. Got a hangover as well. Guess what I… am…doing…now?"

Tiara could hear relaxed breathing at the other end of the phone.

"Meditating?"

"Close. I am getting a massage. Right in my bedroom. It's awesome. Feel so relaxed. Can you hear me breathing?" Scarlett inhaled and exhaled deeply.

"You lucky girl. And guess what a girl like me will be doing now?"

"I can't think of anything", The smooth voice echoed.

"Clean up the mess in the bathroom I created last night. Hanging up. You enjoy your massage"

"Wait"

"What?"

"Today...you remember, don't you?"

Tiara paused for a second. What was she supposed to remember?

"Today, you'll be going with Boris. Don't forget"

Tiara had indeed forgotten that. Boris had asked her to come at five in the evening to a specific address. It will be a forty minutes' train ride from her place.

"Thanks for reminding me. It had slipped my mind", Tiara said apologetically.

"Good luck"

Scarlett disconnected the phone.

An hour later, Tiara, after cleaning up the bathroom, finishing her shower and lunch, still had plenty of time. She was not able to decide on how to spend the rest of the afternoon. Finally, she thought of catching up with a Netflix series on her phone. Lying on her bed, she watched two episodes, before her alarm rang reminding her it was time to step out. Dressed in ripped black jeans and a gray tee shirt and her eyes covered with the sunglasses she had purchased at a discount from

Camden, Tiara was all prepared for an adventure. As planned, she phoned Boris to inform him of the start. Boris was expecting the call, "You ready?"

"I am", Tiara said excitedly.

"Once you reach the address, you will notice a white Toyota waiting at the lane just adjacent to the house. You will find me inside"

"Anything else?"

"Yes. Bring a mask along with you?"

"A mask? What mask?"

"A regular mask. Did you not use a cloth mask during covid?"

"I did. Why will I bring a mask? No one is using anymore"

"Just bring it. I will tell you later why"

Boris disconnected the phone.

The train ride was long and monotonous. Tiara, standing through the entire journey, could not help thinking how she was truly feeling excited to be a part of something underground, unreal and possibly unlawful. What would mum have said knowing the story?

The house was about a fifteen minutes' walk from the station. Once she reached the location, she could spot the white car, waiting as mentioned by Boris. While walking towards the car, Tiara glanced at the house. It had a brick exterior that had faded over the years of rain and sunlight. The front door was painted recently with a dark green color. All windows were closed. Was the person not at home?

Tiara sat in the passenger seat. Boris was wearing a pale-yellow full hand shirt tucked well at the waistline. Tiara thought there could not have been a better shirt to be ignored on the street. It was a thoughtful choice by Boris.

"What's next?" Tiara asked.

"Here is the plan. We go to the door and knock. When he opens the door, I do the talking. We are coming on behalf of Mr. Paulo Carvalho. You don't say a word unless he asks you. Please, it's very important. You just watch what I do"

"And…what are you going to do?"

"I will convince him to admit his crime. And something of that sort. Then we leave"

"What if…he doesn't agree?"

"There are ways"

"Like?"

"I threaten him. If he attacks me, I attack him back. We have a brawl"

"Are you serious?"

"Why will I not be serious? I have done this before many times"

"You actually have beaten up people at their home?"

"Not always at home. But yes, at home too"

"How are you not in prison yet? This is a crime"

"Nobody reports a case like this. Here is the thing. We go with our faces covered with masks. Even if the house has surveillance cameras no one would recognize us. Even if they did, we would say that we came to discuss the crap we just planned. The guy lost his temper, attacked us. We just defended ourselves. That's our alibi. He will not be able to prove his side of story by any means, because there is no one else at home"

"How do you know that?"

"We have done our research"

"Fantastic", Tiara shook her head.

Boris continued, "Even if by some miracle, the police are convinced of his story, I will be in prison for not more than three months. These are regular brawls that happen all the time. We are not burglars. We would not touch a single thing in the house. But he would know that, once I come out of the prison, I will kill him…definitely. So, he will have to be very careful about going after me. Now let's go"

Boris moved out of the car and Tiara followed. They walked towards the house at a casual pace. Tiara stopped suddenly "One last question"

"What is it now?" Boris was not happy with the interruption.

"What if..." Tiara whispered, "He has a gun?"

"That's impossible. This is not America. Trust me"

As they walked to the door, Tiara felt a chilling sensation all over her body.

Boris said, "Mask" and took out his mask to cover the lower part of his face. Tiara obeyed. Boris said "This is the only benefit of covid. No one is going to doubt your intentions"

He rang the doorbell.

The door opened, where appeared a man of medium size with thick golden uncombed hair and cluttered dirty beard. His eyebrows were so thick that Tiara could not help noticing them. He wore a soccer jersey of white base and blue borders which Tiara could not recognize. Looking at his bulging waistline, Tiara concluded that the man had not been working out lately.

Boris cleared his throat and said, "I am here to meet Mr. Russ Gordon. I have an appointment", to her surprise Tiara noticed that Boris spoke in a regular English accent; his Russianness had just disappeared.

"Are you…"

"Jack Lewis. I spoke to you over the phone", Boris said with a smiling face.

"And this is…", The man looked at Tiara.

"My assistant. April"

"Come in", The man, named Russ, waved his hand

inwards and opened the door completely without a particular expression on his face.

April! Tiara exclaimed to herself. What a lovely name! Who could have told Boris to use that name? Must have been Scarlett. Tiara instantly decided that if she ever had a daughter, she would name the daughter April.

They walked inside. It was a small living room with a large flat screen television hanging right above the fireplace. There was a sofa set around the area; one of them had pillows and a small blanket on it indicating Russ must have been sitting there. On the center table, which was made of rectangular wood, broken at the corners, there was a beer can and a popcorn bowl right in front of Russ's seat. He was probably waiting for a game. Tiara looked around the screen. There was indeed some preparation going on for a game.

"Have a seat", Russ pointed out to the sofa. Tiara and Boris found their places. Tiara looked around the room. There was an abundance of photographs fixed at different parts of the room. They were photographs of his family understandably and many other people too, some of which Tiara could recognize as soccer players. Russ was a traveling fan for sure.

Boris looked at the television and tried to start a friendly conversation, "A Spurs fan are you?"

"A season ticket one. You see mate, this year we got a good team but still can't..." Tiara wasn't paying attention to this boring discussion. Her eyes were scanning through the room, which had decorative items hanging on the walls in addition to the pictures. The wallpaper with yellow background and blue designs on it, had been faded for a long time. Most furniture in the room showed similar age with their rugged condition and rough corners. From her sitting position Tiara could not view the kitchen clearly but it appeared small. With the clear examination of the room, Tiara was trying to estimate Russ's income level.

When she looked back, the two men were still discussing, Russ was saying,

"These pillocks can't get me the afternoon matches. The only thing I can watch on a Saturday is the five thirty matches. You see mate, it was so important today, but I had to cancel my plans of visiting the stadium, because I wanted to meet you", Russ laughed out loudly.

"I am so sorry about that. You should have told me. I could have rescheduled", Boris said apologetically.

Tiara was wondering where his family was and was having a hard time controlling herself from asking that.

"That's alright mate. This is important too. Like I said, we are going to finish ahead of Arsenal this time"

"I'm sure", Boris spoke with assurance.

"Would you like something to drink? A beer maybe?", Russ looked at Tiara.

Tiara smiled and said, "I'm fine. Thank you"

"We're fine Mr. Gordon", Boris joined.

Russ continued, "Rather drab of a Saturday. There's nothing much to do than waiting for this fucking thing to start. My wife went to her parents with my younger one. The elder one lives away. You see mate, I'm free as a bird. I was hoping to mow my backyard today, but I couldn't manage to find any inspiration", Russ laughed again. Tiara was glad that her curiosity about the family was answered.

"Inspiration is what I need. Just a little bit of it. I've been thinking about what I am going to do after I retire. It's not too far away. Just a few more years. I realized that I fucking ended up spending every money that I had already. There's just nothing in my savings"

"I understand. It's a widespread problem in society. We don't realize until we are close to the retirement age", Boris prompted.

"You may be wondering; don't I have a pension plan? But the truth is…that bloody thing will pay peanuts. With everything turning so expensive and people going bonkers all around, one needs solid money to retire. Let me tell you what happened last week. My wife, who is normally quite wise and prudent, told me that she just bought a thing with twenty thousand pounds. Can you believe twenty thousand?"

"What thing...she bought?", asked Boris.

"I don't know mate. It's called Ether or something like that. Remember, at school we learnt that there's no such thing as Ether. But this one seems to be real. She told me it's the future...future of all money and returns on them...are supposed to be quite handsome... really...huge...so to say...and that too just within six months...spurious, isn't it? I've never heard of anything like that. I told her, before I lose my mind, could you, explain in your own words, what you have bought. And guess what, she had no clue. She said...it was something online... through some app. How do you expect me to react? That was our last bit of savings. My elder son took a gap year in Colombia last year. Can you imagine how ridiculously expensive that was? I was truly mad at my wife, we quarreled all night long. Luckily, I don't know how...you called me after two days. It was as if you were listening to me. Now, I don't mind you listening to me, but I hope you have something profitable for me"

"I do, I do. I'm glad the timing was perfect. I can assure you whatever I have is going to benefit you"

"Tell me what you have"

Boris cleared his throat again. Was he nervous? Tiara tried to read his expressions, but they did not reveal what his mind was thinking. Tiara wondered whether Boris was sweating because she found the room warm, like she did in most rooms she had ever visited.

"Mr. Gordon, I'm delighted to announce that you have been selected as beneficiary of a will, where you'll be receiving twenty-five thousand pounds, to your bank account whenever you are ready", Boris smiled wide and raised both of his arms sideways.

"Now, that's real good news", Russ shook his head slowly, "But the question is why? and who is this bloke making me a beneficiary from nowhere?"

"For that you may have to travel back in the memory lane. Do you remember someone named Paulo? Paulo Carvalho?"

"Is that a real name? Why would someone have a name like that? I've heard of Paulo Coelho and Ricardo Carvalho. But who's Paulo Carvalho?", Russ scoffed.

"I understand it's quite an unusual act of charity but let me assure you it's real. The name is real too. And the man behind the name too. Now tell me, do you remember anyone by that name?"

"I don't. Unfortunately. Doesn't ring any bell"

"Well, then, we'll have to try to remember"

"Is that the condition for the will? Do I have to remember him to get his money?", Russ continued laughing.

"Unfortunately, that will have to be the case. You can't receive the money if you don't know him"

"Well then, let me fake it. How about this? He was in my school. In my class. We were the best pals. We played soccer together. We sang the Spurs song together. Will that do?"

"I'm afraid Mr. Gordon, if you want to receive the money, you'll have to take this seriously. This is not a joke. The man is dying. He has prepared a list of people he wanted to donate his money to. It's not a big amount per se but, it's still a token of good gesture…"

Russ interrupted, "No No it is a good money. it could fill up my savings immediately"

"Right. But for that you need to remember him. Do you want to try?"

"Yes I do. I want to remember him. But I can't", Russ looked at Tiara and smiled. Tiara was increasingly reaching her tolerance of patience with this man. He seemed a classic example of a failed middle-aged man.

"Let me give you a hint. You are right. He was in your school"

"You see. I wasn't that far. But what then?"

"Think Mr. Gordon. Work hard. School soccer ground. You broke someone's leg. He was absent for a month. Ring any bell?"

"Fucking hell. It's Paulo. That Paulo. It's him. How could I forget?"

"Glad that you finally remember. So, tell us, what do you remember about him?", Boris asked politely.

"I…I…remember quite a lot now. He was a quirky little loser. Sucked in everything. When he played soccer, we felt he would fly away with the ball. He had a strange body…skinny legs and a big head, like a dodgy alien. We used to laugh at him…all the time. He was a joke. For everyone…the boys and the girls". Russ laughed out again. Tiara shivered with the insensitivity of the man.

Russ continued, "I remember one day I made him run in circles of hundred meters for ten times. He lost his breath that day…and…and I swear…I thought he was going to die…Christ…it was that close. My mates helped him to get back home. Now, that you told me, memories are knocking my entire head apart"

"Were you friends with him?"

"I wouldn't call that friend strictly. It's something different. A relationship which made him shit in his pants like a chicken. We enjoyed that. Every time he saw us, he would try to run to the other side. But some of my mates were lightning quick. We would get hold of that sucker very easily and…"

"Bully him?"

"Oh…we could do that all day. Me, my mates,

sometimes girls. It was all so easy for us. Those were fun days. We were having fun. Did you say he is dying? Why is he dying?", Tiara wanted to condemn him loudly for taking so long to understand that someone was dying.

Russ took another sip from his beer glass while glancing at the television twice. Tiara looked at her watch. It had been only twenty minutes since they came inside. Russ's eagerness for the game to start was making it obvious that he wanted to finish the transaction soon.

"Well, it's a disease. Terminal one. He doesn't have much time", Boris answered.

"Sorry to hear that mate. He wasn't a bad guy. An imbecile I'd say. But certainly not a bad one. I'm glad he wants to share a token with me, although…to be honest with you…I reckon, there must be a catch somewhere. Do you know why exactly he thought of me?"

Tiara noticed that besides the wedding ring Russ had three more rings spread over his fingers. They were made of different stones, one red like a ruby, others were gray. It was not clear to Tiara what type of cult Russ was a part of.

"It's a little more complicated than that. There are terms and conditions that must be met before the money is transferred to your account", Boris uttered the sentences very carefully, as if he was testifying in a court.

Russ leaned backwards and grinned, "There it is. Now we are talking. I knew it...there is a catch...I shouldn't be cock-a-hoop so easily. Why on earth would someone pay me twenty-five grand? So, tell me mate, what are the terms? I can't wait to hear"

Boris cleared his throat again. This was the third time so far as Tiara was counting. Did he have a sore throat? Boris continued, "You basically...will have to admit that you did terrible things to him. According to his wish, you'll have to hold a placard with some writing on it and travel across different tubes for an entire day, sitting on the floor of the tube. If anyone donated any money to you in that process, you would collect that and at the end of the day if it reaches ten pounds, you win twenty-five thousand"

"Fucking hell. Holy Christ. What on earth is that?", Russ's face turned red.

"Don't you want to know what's going to be written on that placard"

"Go on"

"It's going to say, *I am a bully. I tortured people terribly. I hate myself now*"

"What the fuck? What makes him and you think that I was ever going to do that?"

"Because you need the money. You are a person with low moral value...you would do anything that benefits you", Boris said with a straight face. Tiara's heartbeat started racing as the tempers were going north.

"You know what? Just get the fuck out of my home. I've had enough of you. Before I break your legs just get the hell out", Russ stood up, Tiara and Boris as well. Tiara realized that her armpits were already sweating. Boris walked calmly away from the sofa. Then he looked at Tiara and said in a low but commanding voice, "Would you increase the volume of the tele more? The remote is on the table"

Tiara saw the remote control lying on the table. She glanced at the television once and then at Russ who was fuming like a volcano. As she picked up the remote Russ cried loud, "Don't you fucking dare touch my stuff, I am going to…"

Before he could finish Tiara had pressed the volume up button very hard. Suddenly a loud noise of crowd from the stadium filled the room, creating a surreal atmosphere of thousands of people watching a drama unfold. Meanwhile, a punch from Boris' right hand went straight below the left ribs of Russ who was taken aback with the sudden attack. He bent forward holding his ribs. Tiara could not hear his groans as the crowd noise continued. Before Russ could look up Boris landed a hook at the left jaw and immediately a punch from his left hand to Russ's right jaw. Russ was dismantled instantly. He collapsed on the ground with his dangling right arm smashing a flower vase placed at the side table and his head thumping against the cupboard placed right behind the sofa. A couple of photo frames displaying his family pictures crashed on the floor and the glass pieces spread all over. Without wasting any time Boris kicked using his right leg two times exactly at the left side of his ribs again. Russ could not even open his eyes anymore. Blood started flowing from his mouth. With one last kick at his stomach, Boris told Tiara, "Let's get out of here. Don't forget the mask"

15

Boris put on his mask instantly and walked quickly towards the door while Tiara followed. After exiting the door, Tiara had one last look inside. Russ was still down. There was more blood flowing from his mouth. Boris pulled Tiara's hand quickly and closed the door from outside. They walked towards the car as fast as they could. Soon, Boris started the car and moved forward. Tiara's heartbeat was racing very fast, she could feel her body was full of sweat and mind was numb. She was terrified. As the car moved on, Tiara continued glancing at the side mirror whether Russ was coming behind them. There was no one on the street. Boris drove the car swiftly across different lanes which Tiara had no idea about. After a few minutes she had lost her sense of direction. Boris was perhaps making it difficult for anyone following them. Or he just knew an easier way to escape.

Tiara's numbness continued even after she realized that there was absolutely no one chasing them. She could not look at Boris. Her hands, folded together, were resting on her lap.

At a traffic light, Boris took out a packet of chewing gum from the gloves compartment. He offered Tiara but Tiara refused. Boris started chewing.

"How can you stay so calm?" Tiara was about to burst.

"What's bothering you?"

"Everything. For a starter, we left a man bleeding alone in his room. He's going to bleed the whole night. And he's going to die"

Boris chuckled, "He's a strong man. He's going to be up on his feet within an hour. Don't worry"

"How do you know he will not die?", Tiara screamed.

"Because I just know. This is not the first time. People can take in hits. It's not that difficult. I have landed the hits very carefully. He'll have some broken ribs, internal injury at the spleen, a couple of loose or broken teeth…and that's all. He's not going to die. He could spend three months resting and wondering what on earth had happened under his own roof. Oh yes, of course, his confidence will be shattered…for as long as he lives. Do you know how that feels?"

"And the police?"

"He will not dare. I'm telling you. A man like him is an insect to society. They should be crushed. They don't respect the law. They never take help from the law as well. We'll remain untouchable. Mark my words"

"But this is illegal. What you did is a crime. You should be prosecuted for that"

"Do it then. Call the police", Boris focused on the road. Although there was still some time for sunset, parts of the road were already looking dark due to lack of streetlights. There were two lanes, but many drivers were changing lanes in a hurry. Traffic towards the heart of the city on a Saturday evening was understandably busy. Tiara was hoping they would reach close to a tube station where she could leave the car. It was suffocating inside.

Browsing her phone apps to distract herself, Tiara was able to control her mind. Then she decided to meditate for a moment by closing her eyes and performing box-breathing. When she opened her eyes, Boris was still chewing. His hands were resting on the wheel in the two ten formats. Tiara spoke calmly, "You are not a Russian, are you?"

Boris looked at Tiara with a crooked smile. Tiara noticed that his lips had tiny black patches. He was perhaps a chain smoker long ago. Boris said, "My grandfather was from Russia. He moved after the war.

He was also part of the army entering Berlin. A proud soldier. A strong man. He never wanted to go back to Stalin's rule. My father was born and raised here. He had never visited Russia. I don't have many memories of my grandparents. I don't even know how to speak Russian"

"Why did you act like one?"

"Because Scarlett asked me to. She wanted to make you comfortable by showing that all of us are not similar. It's called diversity. You know all that shit better than me. It's your generation thing"

Smiling to herself Tiara asked, "Scarlett, asked you to speak in that accent for diversity? Incredible"

"She is incredible"

"I can't imagine how she pays attention to every small detail. She plans everything so well. She tells lies comfortably, manipulates others. Sometimes, I feel, she's weaponizing her situation to achieve something big that none of us are aware of"

"I don't understand whether you are praising her or criticizing. But whatever. To me, she's a waste of talent. Scarlett hasn't done anything with her life. It's a shame. She could do so much better"

Browsing her phone for a minute, Tiara looked outside. Both sides of the roads were now covered by bushes. Road had narrowed a lot. She wasn't sure which way the car was going.

"I guess you are right", Tiara nodded.

"Scarlett is the driving force behind what we do. She's the queen bee on a mission. As if, the burden of teaching a lesson to bullies is lying on her shoulders. If I were Scarlett, I'd live a different life. Anyways, let's forget that. Tell me something Tiara"

"What?"

"Do you want to meet your bully?"

"I liked the way you guys say, your bully, my bully. It's funny. It sounds like they are masters, and we are slaves"

"It's the indisputable truth. We are slaves to them. They had decided the course of our lives. If they didn't exist, we could possibly live a different life"

"You think so?"

"You don't? Look at yourself. The only thing different between you and Scarlett is you don't have a rich father. But otherwise, you too, have no guidance, no ambition…no focus. Do you think…you can live like this your entire life?"

Tiara blinked her eyes two times and looked at the dashboard. What Boris was saying made sense, but Tiara knew that she could not find any answer; not while sitting in this suffocating car and not even when she was lying down on her own bed.

"And look at me. I was on the same boat as you.

But I managed to put myself on the normal flow of life. I've got a family. My son is already working, and my daughter is about to finish her university. I've worked in a mediocre job my entire life. When I look back...I feel...maybe...I could have done better. A little more confidence, attention span, better atmosphere, care, encouragement...I missed all that. And that's because of...like we call them...my bully. Tell me, how did you feel when you saw that son of a bitch biting the dust today? You'll have to be honest"

Boris's words were flowing like music in Tiara's ears. She was speechless for a moment. Then she said, "If I am being honest, I have to say that it was a horror but satisfying. The man was arrogant, disrespectful, and insensitive. He had no repentance of what he had done. I'm absolutely delighted that he was beaten up"

"Our actions are curate's egg. The bad part is we are hurting people but the good part...is more rewarding. When we see these guys receiving a tiny punishment, we feel delighted. In reality... what we did to this guy, is not comparable to what damage he had caused to Paulo. It's about someone's life against merely a few broken ribs"

"What's Paulo's story?"

"It's in the book. You'll have to read it there", Boris grinned.

"Of course. That goddamn book"

Their car had entered the southern part of the inner city now. Streets were flooded with lights and a cheerful crowd whirling around at both sides. There were smaller circles of people in front of the pubs, queues near the restaurants, buses lining up, taxis trying to maneuver; suddenly the world outside their window had been resuscitated.

"That's why...", Boris continued, "I'm telling you. Meet your bully. If you want one of us to go first, let's plan it. Trent will figure out a way. If you find your bully already battered in her life, you'll be happy. It's a priceless feeling. Trust me"

To avoid answering, Tiara browsed her phone quickly and then said, "How about you? Are you happy? Do you enjoy thrashing people like this?"

"Me? I want to run away from this city. Let me be completely honest with you...I just want to leave... everything that I do here. I haven't visited too many places in Europe...let alone the world, but I liked a place in Portugal. It's by the sea. When my kids are out, I want to go away. It's between you and me, I am already looking for a small home there. It's not perfect, a lot of renovation will be needed but it's what I wanted, my wife wanted. And guess how we found it...A Place in the Sun! Never thought it works in real life. When the home is ready, we're going to move there, just my wife and me. We want to be at some place where no one knows us, no one is coming after us. I am fatigued Tiara. This burden is heavy. Very heavy"

"So your wife knows about all these"

"Not completely but she's aware that I've been part of a couple of such actions. She was generally supportive but, lately, she's afraid that cops will come after me. She wants us to run away"

For a moment Tiara was saddened by Boris' situation. Then she said, "This life of yours. You, Scarlett, Trent and others may be thinking that you are doing some sort of service to the world… by hunting down old bullies and punishing them…but let me tell you, you must introspect. Look at yourself in the mirror. Ask yourself, what you've become. Is that what you wanted to be? Did you really want to break into someone's home and beat him up into a pulp? With your act, you are no longer the victim"

"I know what you're saying. When we break into their homes and threaten them, we are the bullies. Not them. It's not always that way though. They guy today, was a real nasty piece of work, but in general, I agree with you. We are acting like bullies. But you think about it, there's no other way to punish them."

"You didn't have to punish anyone. You just had to

move on. Like millions of other people in the world. They have moved on. Revenge is a waste of time. It takes away valuable years of your life. When you look back after many years, you feel like you've wasted a large part of your life and there's no time to correct anything anymore. You wanted to live a happy life with friends and families and achieve your dreams. Instead, you had spent days and nights planning to attack someone who no longer exists in your life. Digging into the unpleasant past can only throw sludge on a rather shiny present. Don't you know that?"

Boris maintained a silence. He looked pensive. His mind was trying to process Tiara's words.

At last, he broke the silence, "At one point, when I started this, I was in for a penny, in for a pound. But I am quite old now. Like I said, I'm going to retire by the beach soon. There'll be no city, no meetings with these people, no adventures. My story is towards the end. But I am truly worried about Scarlett. I really am. I can't see how she is going to live the rest of her life. She has already been suicidal twice. What if she doesn't survive the third one?"

"I know", Tiara said promptly "She needs help"

"She needs help, she needs love...a lot of love, more attention from her family. She needs a true friend, and I can see you could be that friend. I think you should try to pull her out of this; by whatever means. If you must talk to her father for that, so be it. Pursue her, beg her, do whatever is needed. Take her to America to her father. She needs to leave this circle. I can see she is dying...slowly but surely"

Tiara blinked again. He was right. Scarlett was the one who needed help. Not the victims of the stories.

"You care for her a lot, don't you?", Tiara asked.

"Most of us do. She's gone through a lot in her life. We want to see her happy. How about you? What do you think of her?"

Tiara paused. Someone in her school, she didn't remember exactly who, once had said that Tiara, could process events like the frames of a movie in her mind before making a quick decision. It was nevertheless an inspiring statement to her, and she had tried applying it many times in her life. She remembered, particularly the situations where she had to quickly escape Stella's gang by making a choice among several different options and their consequences learned from the past experiences. Sometimes, her methods were effective. Sometimes, they landed her into disasters.

Running a quick check in her mind, Tiara could see two little girls; one with swollen eyes after endless cry, was still waiting for her mother to return or her father to protect her; another, shivering from fear, hiding wherever she could to save herself from torture, because she already knew that her mother wouldn't be helpful, and her father didn't even exist. The former grew up as eccentric, depressed, suicidal woman who loved travelling, reading and writing when she was not possessed by her past; while the latter, turned into a failure who lost concentration easily, broke promises, lacked trust, determination and confidence. The former was privileged in luxury of leisure and comfort while the latter had to stare at gorgeous showrooms only from the glass windows. The former, Scarlett, had everything but could lose the whole world any day and the latter, Tiara, had nothing but was trying hard to overcome her limitations.

Tiara sighed, closed her eyes and said "Yup. I like her too"

16

Sitting on her bed, Tiara opened her laptop to begin her project. As Jacob had said, it needed to be unique, highlighting a topic that was hitherto unknown but relevant to the current society. Tiara had been forming her story over the past few days and today evening had provided her a perfect example of activities that had been going on underground for the last few years. Or was it more? What if there were more groups like what Trent was running? What would be the best way to get her story out so that everyone read it? On the other hand, what would happen if the editors didn't like it? What if Jacob's proposal was outright rejected?

Tiara closed the laptop and put it aside. Anticipation of another failure weakened her nerves. She closed her eyes. This must be her last chance in life. She couldn't think of how it was possible to receive a rare opportunity to offer a story to a newspaper, without any background or a degree. It was all Jacob's influence and Tiara needed to respect that effort. It needed to be a great story. The clock was ticking; it was now or never for Tiara.

The next few minutes were busy as she continued typing the characters, incidents, some comments and statements that she remembered. It was almost nine at the clock when Scarlett's call rang her phone.

Scarlett asked, "How are you holding up?"

"I am doing just fine", Tiara said.

"So, you think…it was, okay?"

"It was not okay. Thrashing someone into a pulp in his own home…is not okay. It's illegal Scarlett. You know that", Tiara said with a grunt.

"But it felt good. You said that to Boris"

"Did I?"

"Well, tell me the truth. How did you feel when you saw the man in blood?"

"I was fucking scared. And numb. And mad. I didn't know why I was there. Why are you doing this Scarlett? Why are you in a constant war?"

Scarlett smiled with her breath. Tiara could hear her sipping from a glass. It must have been one of those fine martinis she occasionally prepared for herself. Scarlett released the glass from the grip of her lips,

"It's not a war Tiara. It's justice. The man deserved it. And many men and women like them deserved it.

They needed to be punished. And if you are worried about the fight, it's nothing at all. People have done worse than this in our city. We have a very long history of terrifying riots...and violence...gang wars...and... there still are. Our history...your history... is soaked in blood. Have you heard of Teddy Boys?"

"I have but I'm not sure what context you are talking about?"

"You know what I'm talking about. You, in particular...people of your community, must learn history. There was plenty of bloodshed for no good reason for years...and...decades. Here, at least, we're trying to bring on some justice"

Tiara was silent; ought to google Teddy Boys once this call was over.

"Tiara..."

"Am here"

"So, tell me, do you want to see your bully suffering the same way?", Scarlett whispered.

Tiara tried to visualize Stella lying on the floor with blood flowing from her mouth, "No. You are not going to do anything like that"

"Of course. Only if you want to"

"However, I want to visit her. I want to see if there's any change in her. I don't expect any repentance, but people change over the years. I want to see if that applied to her"

"I think…", The glass touched Scarlett's lips and moved away, "that's a good idea. When do you want to visit? I can accompany you till her home. Just to be beside in case you needed anything"

Tiara thought for a moment, "I reckon…I need…a little more time…maybe two weeks from now?"

"Do you know where she lives?"

"I actually do. It's near Abbot Road. I can find the exact address"

"Perfect. So we have a plan. You have a good night, Tiara"

"Hey, one thing"

"Tell me"

"I was thinking, I want to see how you track those guys…I mean, those bullies. How you find them, get to know their weaknesses and all that stuff"

"Now someone is nosy", Scarlett giggled.

Tiara giggled as well, "I really am interested now. Today Boris told me that he already knew the guy was alone at home. How did he know so much?"

Scarlett touched the glass with her lips and dragged it slowly away. Tiara wondered whether she was wearing red lipstick.

"I suppose…", Scarlett said, "Boris spoke to Russel's

wife? I don't know to be honest. Are you seriously thinking of trying this out?"

"Absolutely. You introduced me to the friends...the hunters, now I should be more actively involved. Don't you think so?"

"But you just said you were scared watching the man?"

"I was. I'm still going to be scared if I see the fight. But I could help behind the scenes, like tracking the bully. Can't I?"

"You sure can. Keep in mind, it requires patience, an awful lot of it. Are you ready for that?"

"Try me"

"Alright. Let's arrange a call tomorrow with Trent. He's going to tell us what's next. Until then sweet dreams...night night, hunter"

"Wait..."

"Yes?"

"What's Trent's last name?"

"Houghton. Why?"

"I was just going to check something"

As Scarlett terminated the conversation, Tiara started searching for Trent Houghton. The man had profiles in LinkedIn and Instagram. He was active as recently as the previous week. Tiara realized that she had more work to do before she went to sleep.

Next evening, Trent appeared in a zoom meeting with Tiara and Scarlett. He was sitting in his bedroom with the door locked. Perhaps he wanted to hide the meeting from his wife. In his home environment, the aura of intimidation that Tiara had experienced the first time, was blissfully missing. He looked ordinary.

Trent explained to Tiara about the most important rule of the game. That was to remain extremely secretive and discrete. Everyone must follow the rule. Any sign of betrayal could jeopardize everyone else. The mutual trust that they were able to build over the last few years, was working very well. The gang had so far identified fourteen bullies from the past and seven of them had been punished. When Tiara asked why Boris had claimed he had done it many times, Trent responded saying that Boris mustn't have been serious. Boris had only been involved in two direct combats before. None of the other cases required any physical assault. When Tiara asked how they were executed Trent grinned and assured her she would find out on the way.

A day later, they had the same call again. At the same time.

Trent displayed the picture of a man named Brad Connelly on screen. He was a man younger to Tiara, at least by five years or could have been more. Tiara was familiar with the terms already. She asked,

"Whose bully is this?"

"This is one of the three men who destroyed Ethan's life. Son of Helen"

Silence fell over the online connection. Tiara was wondering what Helen must have gone through over the years. Trent continued, "Helen gave me the names. I've already googled them. This guy is the only one in London at this point. The others have moved to the States after they graduated. Your first task will be to know more about the guy, before even thinking of how we can nail him"

Then Scarlett explained to Tiara how the search must proceed. At first, she should be trying to spot him in any of the popular social media apps. In most apps an account would be required to be in the right circle. Tiara was familiar with Snapchat and Instagram and wanted to search there first. Trent shared an account with her. The account belonged to a woman with id megan_99. Tiara felt goosebumps recollecting the chapter about a mysterious woman named Megan attacking a bully. It was all happening to her and her story, excitement and suspense. After receiving the account Tiara said in the zoom,

"I'm going to follow him as early as tonight"

Trent smirked.

Tiara understood the innuendo, "You're already following him. Aren't you?"

"And now, you should take it over from me"

"What else have you known about him? I don't want to reinvent the wheel"

"Not much. He goes on holidays every month. Yes, every month. Like an escape. And it's always some place in Europe. Sometimes Spain, sometimes Italy, sometimes Austria"

"Who does go with?"

Trent laughed, "One must learn questioning from you. He goes with a woman. And no one else. Always, with the same person. She appears to be his girlfriend, but we can't be sure"

"And this man posts the pictures every month? Really? or is it her account you are following?"

"You see. You exactly know how to dig out information. You're right. Our fake account is a follower of both"

"Do I need to ask you…"

"Solanki. Priya Solanki is her name"

The woman named Priya Solanki was a law student. Tiara discovered her details by googling and the next morning, she spent an hour standing in front of the law college building close to Westminster. It was an awkward waiting hour by occasionally looking at the phone and traffic on the street. She had neither done that nor imagined doing it before. The last time she was waiting for someone sitting in the Starbucks, she was by the side of the law. This time she was an underground operative. She was afraid to miss spotting the woman in a crowd of students but fortunately, was able to recognize the face using the picture in her phone. Priya looked intelligent with a square face. She wore a skirt and carried a backpack. After Priya entered the building, she called Scarlett to inform that she was able to spot Priya. Scarlett congratulated her on successful completion of the first assignment.

Next task was to verify Brad. Close to the evening rush hours, she appeared in front of the building where Brad worked in a tech company. There were plenty of stores opposite to the building making her job much easier. She was able to glance at magazines and evening newspapers while observing the entrance of the building. Brad, carrying a black laptop bag on his shoulder, exited the building around seven in the evening, exactly after an hour of waiting. Brad was tall and well-built as if he worked out in the gym regularly.

Again, she called Scarlett to inform that she had spotted the real Brad.

A day later, she was running out of ideas on how

to proceed any further. She decided to browse the Instagram account of Priya again as Megan. Priya was an extremely active user. There were so many photos that Tiara was about to be overwhelmed, until she identified a pattern among them. There had always been a picture once in every alternate Thursday with a group of women. They appeared to be partying together, late at night. Perhaps she loved going out with her girlfriends regularly. Tiara needed to know whether Brad stayed home during the hours Priya was out with her friends. If he stayed alone then they had just found an opening.

Next day, Tiara waited near Brad's office right around seven in the evening. Brad appeared shortly after that. Then he walked towards the tube station where Tiara followed him diligently. They traveled in the same compartment standing close by. It was remarkably easy for Tiara to follow him all the way to his brown brick apartment in Fulham.

She called Scarlett to let her know the plan. Scarlett offered to share the load. The new plan was for next Thursday when Priya would step out with her friends. Tiara would approximately arrive after ten in the night and wait until midnight for Priya to return. In the meantime, she could also watch if anyone else entered or exited the home for Brad. Scarlett would stay awake to repeatedly check on Tiara.

Following the plan Tiara arrived at the spot opposite to the building where Brad lived. It was as late as ten thirty in the night and Tiara was confident that Priya had already left. She planned to examine Priya's page at regular intervals to confirm the friends were already at the party. The street was extremely quiet with only occasional late-night walks of dog owners guiding their pets. To avoid looking suspicious, Tiara continued strolling from one end to the other of the street, sometimes holding the phone in her ears, pretending that she was talking to someone at the other end. She was wearing the same ripped jeans and top from the day of the adventure with Boris. It was her adventure uniform. Though it was almost summer, the part of the night was creating a chill. Tiara was talking to herself asking why she was walking in an unknown road at an odd hour at night to follow a stranger's activity. Why was it necessary? She could be much happier, like she had always been, sipping a glass of wine while watching something on her phone or on the television. Then she reminded herself that her story must progress soon, and this was an essential part of the story.

After an hour later, all the dog owners went to sleep, leaving only Tiara on the street. Two tall lights at both sides of the street were enough to clear all darkness around her. Still, walking alone on the pavement, marked by a faded yellow paint at parts of its corners, where occasional cigarette butts were scattered, was rather unnerving and Tiara wanted to go home soon.

Two hours later, without any sign of anyone entering or exiting the building, with a pair of sore legs, an aching head and worn-out patience, Tiara was planning to leave the place. Just then Scarlett called,

"How has it been?"

"Been a blast", Tiara told in a sarcastic tone, "Waiting for bloody two hours on a road all alone, for something unknown to happen, is a huge huge fun, let me tell you that"

Scarlett laughed at the other end softly. Tiara imagined she was drinking a martini again. Scarlett said in her silky voice, "Welcome to hunting. You're no longer a police officer who can just walk in anywhere. A hunter needs to wait for the right moment. Like the hunter who waits for a deadly panther all night, or a paparazzi who waits for a celebrity's momentary wardrobe malfunction all day long. We are a different league. Patience is our main virtue"

"Whatever. I'm leaving now. I'll call you tomorrow"

Following day or two, Scarlett and Tiara continued discussing how they could break into Brad's life to find his weakness, but it appeared to be difficult. A week passed when Scarlett reminded Tiara that a visit to Stella was due. Tiara convinced Scarlett that she would need one more week as she was too engrossed in Brad to think of anything else. Another zoom was organized with Trent. After listening to Tiara, Trent nodded,

"Indeed appears to be difficult. He seems to be a reclusive man. There are only two places he can be found…his home and work. There's no way we can break into a home like this, or in his office without knowing anything about his weaknesses"

Tiara said, "But how do we find out anything? We can't even get to talk to him. He's not in a pub or restaurant or shopping mall. We can't follow him to holidays. Can we?"

"Erm…we can't go to his holidays, but we can get hold of someone who could tell us about him"

"Solanki!"

Tiara decided to wait for the day when Priya went to a pub after college was over. It took her three days of waiting until on the third day, Priya with two of her friends from college headed towards the pub at the next block. Tiara entered the pub casually and was able to spot them sitting at the bar. Tiara placed herself two seats apart and ordered a glass of wine.

Thinking of her own situation Tiara was amused.

Only a few months ago, she was trying to find criminals and now she had turned into one. Thinking of Barbara Tiara's stomach cringed. She would be heartbroken knowing what Tiara was doing.

When she turned to the side, to her surprise she noticed that Priya was standing beside her. She could not locate the two friends. Priya was staring at Tiara to start a conversation. Without any delay, Priya accused Tiara of stalking her and threatened to call the police. Tiara had already planned this situation. She uttered the lines she had practiced with Scarlett three days ago.

"My name is April. I'm not any criminal. Please believe me. When I saw you for the first time... I...I... found you extremely attractive. Ever since...I've been thinking of talking to you. I've no other intention. If you want me to leave...I can disappear instantly...but all I wanted was to talk to you...please...for just a little while"

Priya was kind enough to grant permission for that little while allowance, though, she made it crystal clear to Tiara that she was happily straight and was living with her boyfriend. They started discussing traffic, law college and other forms of education. Tiara was anxious about the two friends, but they were not visible anywhere in the pub. Had they already gone home, leaving their friend alone? Priya was eloquent and erudite. She appeared ambitious and had certain dreams for herself. After the first couple of drinks Tiara realized that Priya was starting to be more relaxed. She started speaking about how much she loved playing guitar and visiting concerts. After the fourth drink she was condescending her boyfriend for not joining her in Glastonbury. To Tiara's curiosity she answered that her boyfriend loved living a lonely life. He was a workaholic and a fitness freak. When he was not working, he spent hours in the gym. He avoided people. Tiara asked, "That's strange. You mean there are no friends?"

"Absolutely no one. He's all alone. His social media accounts are empty. No one is connected to him. I have a bunch of close friends, but he doesn't let 'em come inside our flat. Can you imagine how rude that is? But that's how he has been"

"Since you know him?"

Priya shook her head, "Yes. Despite all that, I liked him. Our mums had gone to the same school. They were connected recently and when we all met, he was polite and gentle to me. As such, I don't have any complaints. He loves me like I am his universe. I respect that. The only trouble is…"

Tiara was waiting with a rising level of anxiety.

"The only trouble is, he's alone. He doesn't trust anyone else. As if he's hiding from a past. Sometimes, at night when I open my eyes…I see him sitting on the bed staring at nothing. I get terrified. What if there's something wrong with him? What if he had a terrible past? He never answered any such questions. Whenever I asked him, he just said he was under severe stress at work. But…I think…it's much more than that. He's running away from something and that's why he can't sleep at night. We go on holidays every month. He loves that…holidays are great bonding for two of us, away from this hustle and bustle. He prefers being secluded, with just me around"

Tiara remained silent while Priya gulped more drink, "And you know why I'm telling you all these? Because you're never going to judge him. You don't know him. You are a complete stranger"

After going home Tiara dialed Scarlett. Several thoughts were trying to spin more yarns in her mind but she wanted to give it a break for now. Clearly, Brad's story needed more time. While that continued, she wanted to visit Stella. Scarlett gladly agreed to accompany her on the next Sunday evening.

17

A week passed by, with Tiara being busy preparing for her report. She had to recollect all questions and their answers she had been gathering over the last few weeks with different people involved. The material piled up, more and more, waiting for her to thread them together. And just like that, the next Sunday arrived. When the gloomy sky was covered by a bunch of angry dark clouds and her entire neighborhood was locked inside, watching Sunday television programs or movies or Netflix, Tiara, dressed in purple Bodycon and heels, was waiting outside her building for Scarlett. She was conscious initially of the dress being too fashionable for a visit to Stella. That was the best dress she had in years. Thinking again, she was able to shrug the concern off. She needed to look her best in front of her old enemy; she needed the swagger.

Soon Scarlett arrived driving a yellow Beetle. Tiara

had never sat inside a Beetle before. It appeared small for two people. After making herself comfortable she looked at Scarlett who was wearing a sunglass with her hair straightened. She looked sharp and sultry.

"I had no idea you had a car!" Tiara exclaimed.

"It's quite handy. Especially when I want to go for long drives, all by myself. It's great. Works well", Scarlett started the car.

"You got parking in the building, don't you?"

"It came with the flat"

"Where do you go for long drives?"

"It depends. Sometimes highlands, sometimes to the sea. Depends on my mood"

Tiara wanted to stop the conversation. She was feeling envious. She heard somewhere that every girl wants to become like her mother. Tiara never wanted to be like her mother. Barbara's loneliness, void eyes, ruthless duty at the operation theaters, were all part of her memories while growing up. The last thing she wanted was to drink on her own bed when there was nothing else to look forward to. Did Scarlett ever want to become like her mother? Was it all about finding the right person her mother loved? Wasn't there any emotion for her own child? Human actions are incoherent quite often when they are driven by primitive laws of nature. One of the few characteristics that made humans special, was the ability to attach themselves emotionally to other humans or random objects. What was Scarlett's mother attached to?

Their car moved forward through the sparse traffic of Sunday evening. Most pedestrians were holding black umbrellas to protect themselves from the drizzle. Under the streetlights, umbrellas looked like mushrooms covering the streets and their car was trying to find its way inside that wonderland.

About half an hour later, when the car reached Stella's house Scarlett positioned the car close to the next block. Drizzle had stopped and there was absolutely no movement from anywhere in the lane. While the streetlight was missing, a few faint rays of light coming out of the windows of the next house, provided a grisly appearance all around.

"From here it's yours. Best of luck", Scarlett pressed Tiara's hands with her own.

"I'm nervous…a bit I think", Tiara breathed two times thinking that could ease her down, "Could you come with me?"

"No Tiara. This is your moment. You're going to do great. Don't worry. Now go"

Tiara walked in the lane. The air smelt of fresh rain and breeze. Taking another step forward, Tiara could see the number on the building. Walking up the stairs to the main door, Tiara found that there were door numbers to choose for the bell. It was easy enough to reach Stella.

Tiara breathed again and rang the bell.

Stella opened the door even before Tiara finished counting thirty. Tiara stared at her for a minute. Stella was big, as before but her face was worn out due to lack of care. Her hair was tied behind but even with the pale light near the door, Tiara could see that the hair was not in the best of condition. Stella wore glasses as well. Tiara could not recollect Stella wearing glasses before.

Stella was observing the stranger at the door. Her effort to search in the memory lane continued for a good number of minutes. Finally, she cried loudly, "Tiara…"

"It's me, indeed", Tiara smiled nervously.

"Come in come in", Stella walked inside, and Tiara followed. It was a very small room, not even half of the room of Russ Gordon. The room had a pale paint, almost faded to colorless patches at different places. There was a flat screen television in front of the sofa, where two little boys of about the same age, wearing the same blue colored shirt and white shorts were watching some channel on YouTube. Adjacent to that area, there was a kitchen where dishes and plates were piled up. The family must have just finished their supper.

"Off to bed boys, no more tele", Stella commanded.

The boys switched the television off and walked towards the next room, glancing at Tiara from the corners of their eyes. Tiara presumed that was the bedroom. Stella quickly dusted the sofa and indicated to Tiara to sit there, "Can I get you something?"

"Nothing at all. I am…not going to take much of your time. I apologize for walking in like this. It was totally unplanned", Tiara was embarrassed already. It was probably a bad idea to come here. She had just disturbed a rather regular Sunday evening of this family.

"No please. Don't say that. You have no idea how happy I am seeing you. It's been so long. How long do you remember?", Stella was smiling. Tiara could see a glow in her eyes.

"Seven years? or ten? I don't remember exactly"

"How have you been? How did you find my address? It was such a great surprise. I wasn't expecting anyone. No one comes to visit me. Let alone a Sunday evening and when it's raining. I was thinking who could this be? And I was so lucky today. It's so good to see you Tiara"

After Stella paused, Tiara said, "I'm doing okay. I still stay at mum's. Since we moved out of…" A sad memory was trying to erupt but Tiara was able to suppress it, "Mum still kept in touch with some of those ladies. One of them knew where you lived. When did you move here?"

"That's a long story. First you tell me about you. What do you do? Did you get married?" Stella folded her legs on the sofa to sit comfortably. Tiara noticed that Stella's fit was dry and cracked at many places.

"I'm not married yet. Like I said, I'm staying with mum. She needs help. She's getting old"

"Is she still with the NHS?"

"She is. Still at the operation theaters. Nothing has changed in her life. I work for a newspaper", Tiara realized that she told a lie for the first time in ages. Was it the influence of Scarlett?

"That's great. You are established", Stella smiled big and said "And look at me" she scoffed dry. Tiara did not return any gesture. It was not going well.

"Your boys are cute. How old are they?" Tiara needed to ask something nice.

"They are eight. Remember…I was carrying them when you left the old home?"

To avoid any eye contact with Stella she turned her phone screen quickly to pretend she was expecting a message. Then she said, "I remember"

"And don't say they are cute. They are murderers. I'm always scared to leave them alone anywhere. I think I'll go crazy very soon"

Tiara smiled faintly, "It must be great to have so much joy at home. Where's your husband?"

"In prison"

Tiara laughed, "Good one. Married life huh. He feels it's prison"

"No, I am serious. He is in prison. Since the last five years and will be there for many more years", Stella spoke in an emotionless expression.

"I'm so sorry. What exactly happened?"

"He was working in the Woolwich dock. I met him online and we liked each other instantly. Everyone was okay with me getting married...even before I finished any decent education. So... we did. Then we had the twins...actually...it was much before the wedding...I got pregnant. The twins were our angels. Ours was a small life...we had struggles with daily needs, but we were a happy family. Then one day, he was arrested. Charges were severe. He was part of some gang that operated at night, and he apparently had stabbed someone. I couldn't believe how that could be possible. That night, he said he was going to work, and I remember correctly...when he had returned home in the morning. He would never lie to me about what he was doing. Someone else was behind the whole thing and they used him as a scapegoat", Stella stopped to breathe.

Tiara moved closer to Stella by pushing herself forward, "That is insane. Did you not try to fight the case?"

"I tried but there was a whole bunch of evidence against him that proved him guilty very easily. I still didn't understand why someone ganged up against him or set him up. How a month of turmoil had changed everything. He went to prison. We had no savings. I had no job, no degree, no skill but to feed two small children"

"I'm so sorry to hear that"

"That's alright. It's not your fault. You know how I was able to survive in the end? A friend introduced me to a cleaning agency owner. The gentleman was kind enough to offer me the job. He took a large cut initially from my pay but eventually I was able to demand better. You would think Stella is now cleaning homes and that's so embarrassing…"

Tiara protested immediately, "No I'd never think that. Every job has its dignity"

"That's not how my parents thought. They hated the idea of me getting into cleaning other homes. I told them these are costly homes of rich people. You might have seen them as well when you drove past these sides. The tall buildings with glass windows. Many flats remain empty. Owners live in Russia or China or some countries like that. The management schedules monthly cleaning. It's good money"

"I was just going to ask you. Why didn't your parents help you?"

"They were planning to pull some money for me, but right then, another tragedy hit me. They were deported back to Guyana"

"What?" Tiara could not believe her ears.

"It's a dubious scam. Thousands of people like us were identified as illegal as there were no papers that proved when and how their ancestors had migrated. My father always said that the system was built on trust. People had migrated by many different means. Not everyone carried a proof. But this time, rules were strict. They tracked down many people who arrived decades ago and just sent them back"

"Holy cow. That's so unfair. Did you try to fight and bring them back?"

"I wasn't able to. I had too much to manage myself. My children were little. I didn't have any support or money. Those couple of years were rough on me. But I have plans to bring them back. My father had started gathering money from there to arrange a return. Meanwhile, the pandemic started. Everything halted. Cleaning company started losing business as there were restrictions to enter the buildings. There was no income for months. During the hard lockdowns, I stayed home with the kids. I can't tell you how difficult that time was.

Thankfully, things came back to normal…I'm doing okay…much better… now. I still clean homes and I am planning to bring my parents back"

Tiara wanted to hide somewhere in the room. It was difficult to continue looking at Stella. Tiara came here to meet a different Stella who was strong, aggressive, notorious and ruthless. Instead, she met someone demolished to the ground by the sheer struggle of existence. Tiara wanted to remain the victim. She could not bear the role of the privileged. That was not what she had in her mind.

"Can I get you something to eat Tiara? We still have some peas left if you want. Today is Sunday as you know. I'm sorry I didn't know you were coming…we just finished our supper…" Stella said apologetically.

"No…no…I…really should be going. I was going to some other place nearby…then it came to my mind that you live here. So… it was just a curious visit", Tiara stood up and motioned towards the door, "I'm going to visit another time, to spend more time with you. But, today, I really have to go"

"Do you have my phone number? You can call me anytime if you want to visit"

As they exchanged the phone numbers they walked out of the door. Tiara said, "It was really nice meeting you Stella after so many years…"

"I'm grateful to you that you visited my place. No one really comes here. We haven't had a visitor for a few years now. You really surprised me. Thank you so much"

Before Tiara could take the steps down, Stella whispered, "Tiara..."

Tiara turned back. Stella was standing at the door with both hands trying to break knuckles at each other.

"I…"

"Yes Stella, tell me"

"I wanted to apologize to you. I had been thinking for years but didn't get the courage to meet you. I guess I could have taken the initiative…but I wasn't brave enough. Now that you are here, this is my chance"

"Apologize for what?" Tiara asked softly as if the children were trying to eavesdrop from the bedroom.

"For how I treated you when we were young…I was a bad bad person…everyone would agree. I didn't think about what I was doing. I lived for my happiness. I didn't care to understand how you were suffering…I was selfish…a terrible monster…a bully", Stella's voice started to break. Looking at her eyes under the bulbs hanging above the door, Tiara could see tears dropping from both sides.

"Please…please forgive me…Tiara…", Stella's voice stopped. Tiara stepped forward and embraced Stella. Her body was warm and waiting to be cuddled.

Moments later, Tiara was walking towards the car. She continued looking back after every two steps to find Stella still standing at the door. Inside the car, Scarlett was reading something in her phone. Tiara sat on the passenger seat and fastened the seatbelt silently without looking at Scarlett.

"Do you want to cry?" Scarlett asked with her silky voice that she saved for such special moments.

Tiara nodded silently.

"Tissues are in the gloves compartment. I'm going to drive towards the observatory park. You've got about fifteen minutes to vent your tears out"

"Why are we going there? Gates will be closed"

"Don't worry. We'll find a way"

18

Scarlett maneuvered the car from the small lane out while Tiara started weeping gently. As the car raced through the empty streets and a deserted tunnel, Tiara consumed tissues and lost track of how much time they had been driving. That fifteen minutes passed by rapidly and soon Scarlett was driving at a slower pace as the lanes became narrower. Finally, she parked the car at the corner of a lane. They walked out in the dark street.

"Come with me", Scarlett took Tiara's hand and walked towards a small lane that appeared to be leading towards the backside of the park. Walking effortlessly as if it was her backyard, Scarlett could manage to get them through. Tiara realized that Scarlett knew the place extremely well. Soon, they were under a large tree with a tiny walkway behind them and the glittering view of the stunning city skyline was in front.

"This is not allowed, Scarlett. We are not supposed to be here at this hour"

"Just relax. You just don't know how to relax. Let's sit here for some time. At least, until we get caught by the cops. What do you think?" Scarlett giggled and sat down under the tree. With her hands balancing her body backwards, she stretched her legs on the grass. Tiara had little difficulty sitting down with her dress, but she felt relaxed sitting on the grass.

Time stopped around them. Silence wrapped Tiara's mind all around. Fresh air filled her lungs. With her eyes closed, she wanted her body to dissolve into the vacuum.

"May I ask you something Tiara?" Scarlett broke the silence after a few minutes.

"You want to know why I cried, don't you?" Tiara spoke in a dry voice. She realized that she wanted to drink some water.

"So tell me. Why did you cry?"

Tiara stretched her legs completely and bent her body down so that she could lie down on the grass, facing the sky above. Scarlett followed the same and laid down beside her. Placing her hands on her belly Tiara continued, "I am...always...the one who is used to playing the role of a victim. When it comes to the people from my childhood, I expect them to say to me...oh

Tiara, I feel so sad for you…how your life was messed up, and I…and I…always, felt a hidden pleasure considering myself as someone who could have lived a much better life, only if the circumstances around were favorable. Then I met you, and…and then the other guys. Read some of their stories. I heard your story. All that started to make me feel much better…in a good way. I no longer felt alone. At the same time, I realized that I was losing my victim status. It wasn't a bad thing, but it was new to me. When I went to Stella…I expected her to be the same person as before…so that I could just go back home, consoling me that the villain is still out there. But who I saw was a devastated woman. She had gone through a remarkably difficult time. I couldn't stop thinking how I would have struggled to survive in her situation. It's her bravery that paid off. I cried because I realized that she had a superior soul than me. She fought back extreme circumstances. She never gave up her battle. I cried because she apologized to me for everything, she had done to me. I cried because we are helpless creatures without any control of what can happen to our lives. Stella has received her punishment. A way more punishment than any of us could have offered"

Scarlett uttered, "hmm. How do you know she wasn't lying?"

"Lying for what?"

"To receive some sympathy maybe?"

"No way. She was genuine"

"It doesn't happen normally. These bullies live normal happy lives and one day people forget they were bullies"

"Perhaps, we need to look deeper in their lives. Everyone has a story and, in that story, somewhere, at some point, they must have lost their battle. Who knows? We already heard the story of Brad. He's broken. He can't even sleep at night. And how many years have passed since the incident? Isn't that a great punishment? Karma exists and just like Brad and Stella, everyone else must have faced Karma at some point."

"Karma is a lazy bitch. She needs a nudge to move. We are that nudge"

"You are running behind revenge. It just prolongs your own suffering. What we went through was a phase of our lives and we learned a lot from that. Likewise, everyone must have gone through phases. You should stop looking through the blue lens. It's not too late"

"Too late for what? To give up what I've been doing? I told you I have a purpose. I want to change the world to a better place. I want to create awareness. The world we live in is heavily connected. It's easy to move people online, even though they're nowhere near you. We can bring a change. We can stop people from hurting each other"

"How about yourself? You tried to kill yourself remember? How could you do that? Why was it so easy to end your own life?"

"It wasn't easy. I told you that...didn't I?"

"But you had the thought. What if you want to do it again?"

"I won't do that again. I told you that too"

"It's not good enough Scarlett...not nearly good enough. You need to get organized. You still have time. You could go back to school...complete higher studies. Work in some constructive career. Or just move to America, close to your father"

"Why are you telling me all these? Are you, my mum?" Scarlett's voice was polite but sharp.

"I'm telling you because I see you wasting your talent. It's a huge huge waste. You are the daughter of a successful banker. You must have received some talents from him. You could...at the very minimum, study a lot, an awful lot...until you get a job that makes you happy. You could still change the world. Work at spare time to create awareness, new religion. But at present, what you're doing...in the name of bully hunting, is hurting you...killing you in turn. Listen to me Scarlett. You can't let your life waste like this. It's not too late. You could still move out before something worse happens"

Scarlett did not respond. They continued lying

259

down without looking at each other or their watches or phones. Staring at the illuminated skyline Tiara wondered if they could take shelter in a new home in a completely different corner of the city and forget about the entire world, starting from tonight. She wondered what Scarlett was thinking. She could never get hold of Scarlett's mind effectively. There were still dark corners which were impossible to reach. Suddenly, Scarlett broke the silence, "Are you going to follow what you're saying?"

"Follow what?"

"You just told me that I should start fresh…a new career, new perspective. Are you going to do it yourself?

"I want to. After I met Stella today, I've realized that I've been wasting my presence by crying over my past. It makes no sense. I need to be like Stella. Keep going even in the worst condition. I'm going to try my best to get the job at Jacob's office. If that doesn't work, I'm going to go back to study. Work hard. A girl of my age, shouldn't be treading water like this"

Scarlett turned over on her stomach and looked at Tiara, "I want to start a new life too. But I…am scared. When I'm alone and nights are long and I don't have anything to look forward to, I dive deep into my memories. That brings me down to the lowest point I can think of. There were times, I stood in front of my glass window and just scratched them because I felt the city was trying to intimidate me. I'm always under constant fear of being left alone. Between me and happiness, there's a long winding road"

Scarlett turned to her earlier position again. Tiara placed her hand over Scarlett's and said "You'll not be alone. What if we plan it together? You go back to school, and I start working. We could rent a small new flat. Your school during the day and my work. We come back in the evening, cook together, drink, party out, movies, drive…whatever we like. What do you think?"

Scarlett sat up and folded her legs to her chest, "Will you really do that for me? Will you leave your mum and move in with me?"

"Why not?" Said Tiara, "I've done that before. Mum would be happy watching me moving on with a new beginning"

Scarlett stayed quiet. Almost a minute later, Tiara heard her sobbing. Her face was buried in her knees.

"You okay Scarlett? Did I say something wrong?"

"You did not say anything wrong. I'm just worried thinking all these nice words…that you are saying now…will be wiped out when we go back to our lives tomorrow morning. It happened to me before… every time I thought I was going to be happy…I was hurt in the end"

"But this time will be different. You'll have to believe me. I'm going to make that happen. Let's leave behind all these messes you have created. Let's just take a break first. How about we visit New York? and meet your dad? He'll be really delighted to see you. He's been waiting for years"

Scarlett took a large sniff and then wiped her face with the corner of her top. Then she said,

"You have already thought of all these haven't you? Have you spoken to my father too?"

Tiara did not answer.

"Christ No. You spoke to my father. What did you tell him?" Scarlett's anxiety climbed high.

"Relax. I've not said anything about the bully stuff. Obviously. I just told him that it's time he did something constructive for you besides sending dollars. He agreed that you should go back to school and he's ready to sponsor any money for that. Applying to American universities is not difficult. Lots of students do that. You're a little over aged but it's still not late"

"Oh my god Tiara. This is way too far. You actually… told my father…I can't believe this. What were you thinking?" Scarlett was agitated but her voice was still calm. Tiara thought it was the effect of the magnificent night sky.

"It just came to my mind suddenly that I should call him. So, I did. Last week…"

Scarlett interrupted, "How did he sound? Was he polite to you?"

"He was great. Don't worry. He listened to me patiently. He appreciated that I called him. I'm doing the right thing Scarlett. Let's not discuss it now. When you go back home, sleep on this idea. You can tell me later next week"

Scarlet silently stretched herself again on the grass. Both women continued looking at the sky. After an eternity Scarlett asked, "If I go to an American university, how will you move in with me?"

"Erm…I thought about it. We'll have to work that out. We need to try to get you into a school in a big city where I can find a job. I don't know what job or what work permit will be needed. I'll have to ask Jacob. He knows everything", Tiara smiled to the vacuum above.

Tiara could hear Scarlett humming a tune to herself. She seemed relaxed now. Perhaps the idea of a new place created excitement in her; or it was the prospect of meeting her father. After she finished humming Tiara asked, "Do you trust these guys, Scarlett?"

"Trent?"

"Trent and the others. I don't trust them. They could bust you any day"

"They wouldn't. We're all connected by the same sin. They'll be afraid of that. When I wrote the book, they reviewed it a thousand times. Only after they agreed that all stories were cryptic enough, they were okay to publish it. We're together for a purpose. And they know that very well"

"Did you say the idea behind everything about bully hunting came from Trent?"

"He was the initiator...yes...I think I told you...he was raging with revenge when I met him first time"

Hesitating for a moment, Tiara picked up a grass in her finger and played with it for a little time. Then she whispered, "Did you ever love Trent?"

Scarlett paused for a moment; then said, "I tried. But soon he realized that I was not normal...we started quarreling frequently. I expected he was similar to me, but I was wrong. He was much stronger and determined to execute his plan...and...that was the only motivation driving him"

"Well...in that case...why was he on the dating sites? He was already married"

"Yes he was. That was one of the things driving me nuts...I suppose... he was just checking out options and at the same time trying to find a partner for his crime... if you want to call it a crime"

"So he dumped you?"

"Kind of...he taught me to believe in situationship. A relationship doesn't have to go to any destination. When the situation demanded we were friends or anything else..."

"He's wicked. I already told you..."

"Besides...you'll have to understand...I'm a psycho. When I hit the lowest point, people can't stand me. They run away. It's not easy to love me...and not that I'm ready to love anyone"

Tiara picked up another grass in her hand and started playing with it using her fingers. She wrapped the grass around her finger and asked,

"I remember...you're telling me that...you were guilty that night of something. Were you guilty of poisoning the old man...or something else?"

Scarlett folded one leg on top of the other and said, "You will have to read my book dear. The book will tell you everything"

"You know that I'm not good at reading"

"But that's the only way to know the story"

"Okay okay. Just tell me, which story in the book is yours"

"All stories in the book have names starting with Reign and Fall. It describes a bully's reign and then in the next chapter, it tells how the bully was destroyed.

You'll find just one story which doesn't have the Fall but only Reign. That's my story"

"Why didn't you write the conclusion to your own story?"

"Don't ask me any more questions. Let's go home. You'll have to do the reading"

THE REIGN OF PENNY

Day 1

Penny is my aunt. Her face is long, and eyes can't tolerate nonsense. I thought she loved fun but I was wrong. When she noticed me in the afternoon, building a cave using pillows from the sofa, she yelled at me saying "Don't be a baby". Today is my first day at her place. My father dropped me in the morning and kissed me goodbye. Penny said I may have to adjust by sleeping on the couch as they had no extra bedroom. She has two boys: my cousins. They are excited about me being here, but Penny told them I can't sleep on their bed. My clothes are arranged inside Penny's bedroom. She is going to tell me every day what clothes to wear. I had a red brush for my hair which my mum used before I went to sleep every night. I can't find that brush anymore. The living room feels cold. I don't know how to turn on the fireplace.

Day 20

The room doesn't feel cold anymore. I use the blanket to wrap myself at night. When I need to use the toilet, I carry the blanket with me. But on most nights, I sleep well, without waking up in between, because I am tired at the end of the day. After my school when I return, I help Penny in the kitchen and with cleaning as well. My cousins go out to play. I am allowed to go some days when the work is less, or Penny decides to order Pizza for dinner. In the evening Penny and her husband, my uncle, help my cousins with their homework. I try to finish on my own. Some days, I get it all wrong and my teacher criticizes me. I wanted to ask my father how to improve my homework skills, but Penny warned me not to whine to my father on everything like a baby. He calls me almost every day. I have not told him anything about how I live here. We discussed our plans for a holiday in the mountains. And nothing else.

Day 693

I have grown up a lot.

The little couch in the cold living room is my cozy home now. I continue helping Penny in the kitchen after school. My performance at school is not commendable. My teachers showed concern repeatedly and discussed it with Penny. I am never going to know the results of that conversation. Both my cousins have grown up as well. They don't want to play with a girl like me anymore. They enjoy playing rugby with other boys. I watch television when I am alone.

My father hasn't called for a month. He has reduced his calls lately. New York City has been his home for a year now. He had promised to take me along with him, but I suppose he is too busy for anything. I cried at first, but I don't feel any tears anymore. Our plan for the mountain holidays is still on. My father said cow bells in Switzerland create a special melodious sound. I am eager to hear that, by the side of a green mountain, under a blue sky. From deep inside my heart, I know it's never going to happen because I have learned to be a pessimist over these years.

I have grown up a lot but my soul has been languishing.

Day 824

Last week a man named Roy arrived. He has a very sharp nose, like a bald eagle. Penny told me he is her own brother. Roy needed a shelter for a month and Penny offered my cozy room to him. Roy patted me at the back saying that he would tell me bedtime stories. That was silly. I don't need bedtime stories anymore.

Since then, he has been sleeping on the floor with a

blanket, right beside my couch. At night, I feel his hands touching me, all over my body. If I try to scream, he closes my mouth with his hand. His hands are very strong, I can't even bite them. I cry when he finishes. I have been crying for a week. He told me to keep it a secret or he is going to kill me.

Day 868

Yesterday I told my uncle about Roy as I could not continue anymore. I have been trying to tell Penny about it for many weeks, but she yells at me saying I always whine like a baby. She told me Roy is also my uncle and uncles are often playful. I wanted to discuss it with my friend at school, but I was afraid that if Penny came to know I may be dead.

My uncle, Penny's husband, has shown a lot of concerns. I hope he works on it.

Day 910

Roy was thrown out of home today. Before he got into a taxi, he promised that he was going to kill all of us very soon.

Penny was not happy with me. She has lost her brother because of me. I am hiding under the bed for now. I don't know what to do next. It's going to be a long day before I go to sleep.

19

Radio was playing a series of The Weeknd hits loudly while shadows of trees, with blue sky in the background, were drawing patterns on the car windscreen. Although parts of the roads had bumps, Tiara was enjoying the drive at a high speed. Most stretches on the motorway to her destination, SouthEnd on Sea, had been free of traffic so far, but it was only a matter of time they would hit a busy section. In front of the steering wheel, wearing her sunglasses that added the extra flavor of swagger, Tiara was enjoying the drive to the fullest.

Jacob was looking at his laptop by leaning backward on the passenger's seat. He agreed to help Tiara only on the condition that Tiara was not going to disturb him during the journey, as he apparently had a handful of work to complete. Tiara had promised him that she would listen to the radio, sing songs to herself or simply drive in silence but, under any circumstances, wouldn't ask anything to Jacob. In return, Jacob agreed to join the adventure and cooperate with Tiara's plan.

Pressure from Jacob to complete the article had been mounting since the last few days, making Tiara work late nights to compile the pieces of the report together. She wanted to see the end of Brad's story in order to have more insights on the bully hunting process. Two nights ago, Trent arranged a video call with Tiara and Scarlett again. Tiara didn't have a concrete plan to share, but she insisted on the fact that Brad had already been suffering from trauma and fear. Perhaps, attacking him wasn't absolutely necessary but Trent was adamant; he wanted justice in a more direct manner. Tiara wanted to continue the argument, but Trent was not in any position to listen to anyone. He said that from now on, he was going to handle the mission himself and he didn't need anything from Tiara.

Meanwhile with help from Jacob, Tiara was able to fix an appointment for her next lead. Jacob, as always, was ready to help in order to finish the story soon.

About half an hour later, the GPS showed that they were very near to their destination address. It took her extra effort to maneuver through the narrow lanes and eventually get to the main road that provided a clear view of the sea. There were rows of houses packed by the waterfront. Tiara wondered how costly those houses could be. The address of the bar by the beach soon highlighted on her screen. Tiara had to park the car at the opposite side of the road as most of the parking spots were already occupied. Jacob finally realized that the car had stopped. He pulled the seat straight, folded the laptop into the bag and said, "Here we are. You drove smoothly. I had no idea how time went by"

Twisting her lips to the side, Tiara opened the door. Sometimes, Jacob tries to act overly smart.

As they walked to the bar Tiara could smell the sea and feel the breeze on her skin. Morning sun was almost moving towards the top. Tiara thought she would start sweating very soon.

It was not difficult to spot the old man on one of the outdoor chairs of the bar. He wore a faded blue tee shirt and white shorts. He was holding a glass of beer in his hand.

They walked towards the old man. Jacob waved his hand, "Mr. Baker?"

"Andy. Call me Andy. I like the American style. Use the first name", Andy, the old man in faded blue tee shirt and white shorts, smiled at them.

"I am Jacob, and this is my assistant Tiara. We spoke over the phone" Jacob said courteously and casually presented his identity card towards Andy who, glancing at the card, rapidly nodded his head forward and pointed his hands towards the chairs in front him.

"Fancy a beer?" Andy spoke in a husky voice. Tiara noticed that he had marks around his eyes as if a pair of glasses should have been there. Perhaps, he missed his glasses back home. Andy's skin was crumpled. Tiara thought he wasn't taking care of himself for quite some time. He didn't appear very old; it must have been the effect of stress or sorrow.

Jacob adjusted himself on a chair. Tiara sat on the next one. Looking at the picturesque glittering sea in front of her, with the sun shining from the top and boats floating lazily towards the horizon, Tiara wished she could sit here for the rest of the day or more, like, months or years; just sipping beer and napping occasionally.

Jacob began the conversation, "So Mr. Baker... Andy, as we spoke over the phone, I am creating a report with some of the recent unsolved crime cases. As I read about your wife's case, I was convinced that there could have been some more stories hidden behind it. I'm glad that you've accepted the invitation to talk to us. I really appreciate your cooperation"

Andy waved his right-hand half lifted to indicate there was no need for any formality. Jacob continued, "Would you like me to keep my recorder on or you are comfortable with pen and paper writing only?"

Andy thought for a second. It was clear that no one had ever asked him that question.

"I think the recorder will be just fine. I'm never going to say anything that's not true. Yes, it's fine. Keep the recorder on"

"As you wish sir", Jacob took out a small tape recorder from his bag. Tiara was not aware that at the age of phone apps, journalists like Jacob, were still using old fashioned recorders. Jacob pressed the switch on and said, "You may start now". Tiara wasn't expecting Jacob had planned this step already. She was impressed with his forward thinking.

"My name is Andy. I'm retired. As you can see it's a great day and I'm doing my best to spend my retirement with beer..." Andy was interrupted by Jacob,

"Andy, it's great that you want to speak but the tape is only of a limited size. It will be really really...helpful if you could jump to the point"

"Well, in that case, why don't you ask me the questions you are looking for answers? I really don't know how to do this", Andy was certainly disappointed.

"Tiara, I'd like you to start the questions we have", Tiara was impressed again as Jacob knew she wanted to lead the show.

Tiara cleared her throat and said, "My first question will be, when did your wife pass away?"

"Didn't you say that you read the story already? You're telling me you don't know when it was?"

"I know sir but for the consistency in the recording, please recount", Tiara pleaded.

"It was about a year back. We went to visit a holiday home. It was in Cotswold. We used to go there years ago with our children. We loved to go there. It was affordable, close to home, and had loads of things to do. After they left home, it was just us, me and my wife Penny. We never felt like going there without the kids. But last year…we just visited again. On the second night, Penny apparently had stepped out of the home and a car ran over her. It was around two in the morning. The roads over there are quite isolated, you know… especially at night. Police investigated for one day and declared that the case was an accident…hit and run", Andy exhaled big. Tiara wasn't sure what thoughts were running in his mind.

"What else did the police say?", That was Tiara's next question.

"Well, all ridiculous stuff. They grilled me for an hour asking how come I couldn't hear sounds of my wife stepping outside at that hour? Why was I drunk like a skunk that night? They were stupid. All they could do was to question my drinking. It was my holiday dammit. They also said Penny was not wearing her glasses when the accident took place as they found the glasses beside Penny's bed. It was bizarre why she would step out without her glasses. Police did not think it was. They tried to prove that Penny was drunk, which she was, and so drunk that she had no idea what she was doing"

"So, you think it was not an accident?"

"You tell me. Your boss just said that he decided to make a report on my case. Why so? Why does he think it was an unsolved criminal case?"

Jacob said thoughtfully, "Well, it was just a hunch for me. When I read about it I thought it just wasn't complete"

"That's exactly how I felt as well, standing right in the middle of the crime scene. I am calling it a crime scene because I believe it was a crime scene"

"How old are your kids? Why didn't they pursue any further?" Tiara asked.

"They don't live here anymore. They are busy with their families, jobs and stuff like that. I'd never want to drag them into legal matters...and to be honest with you...their wives were reluctant as well...in fact... everyone accepted that Penny died in an accident. It was...as if... convenient to everyone", Andy gulped the remaining beer at once and signaled the bartender for another. While his glass was being replaced, Tiara asked, "Do you suspect anyone?"

"I do. Of course I do. I am pretty sure it was Roy who killed her"

Tiara waited for Andy to continue explaining who Roy was. Andy was not in a rush. He wiped the mouth of the glass with a tissue and then had a sip, "We'll have to be careful about what we are taking in the mouth. You can never be sure how Covid attacks you"

Ignoring that Tiara asked again, "Would you like to tell us who Roy was?"

"Oh Roy. He's my brother-in-law. Penny's own brother"

"And...? You are saying he killed his own sister?"

"He is capable of killing his own mother as well. He's a deranged man...a lunatic…a seasoned criminal. He had multiple offenses in the past…and I heard one of them was of a rape. I wasn't sure whether he broke a jail, or the cops could never arrest him. Nevertheless, I always disliked him...and the feeling was mutual from his side too"

"But why would he kill his sister?"

"It's a long story. Would you like to hear it?"

"Absolutely sir. That's why we're here", Tiara said.

Sipping from the glass again, Andy began, "It all started with Veronica, my sister. The most beautiful woman I have ever come across. She was even more beautiful than my mother. She was the pride of our family. I tell you she had so many boyfriends that I had lost count. One day…she told our family that she was going to marry an American man. The man worked in a bank. We met him soon. He was a trim and tidy gentleman who meant business. He wore branded luxury watches and gorgeous suites. I felt embarrassed standing in front of him. I was a nobody. Anyhow, Veronica was content with her married life. She started looking like a diva… with all her expensive designer clothes and accessories. Soon I was married, and Penny arrived. She never quite tolerated my sister. I believe she was jealous of my sister's life. Penny often expressed grievances near me…about Veronica's arrogance, criticized her character's flamboyance and free spirit and even called her a whore multiple times…you know…sometimes, Penny was quite uptight. She wasn't exactly like that when I first met her…but, when it came to Veronica…Penny hated everything related to her… Penny believed strongly that my sister would end up in an extramarital affair and I remember arguing with her that Veronica loved her husband a lot…and one day, proving me wrong…Veronica disappeared. Just like that. No one, including her husband, had any clue that she was having an affair. The family and friends…were rattled by the incident…but Penny was delighted. I still remember her repeatedly reminding me how she had read my sister's mind so well. Veronica had a daughter, named Scarlett, who was about ten years old then. I was mortified by her sorrow. Out of courtesy, I offered her father the idea that my family could keep Scarlett with us… taking care of her for a few months or maybe a year…while he got himself arranged. Penny opposed it immediately. However, to my surprise, Scarlett's father agreed…and so Scarlett moved in with us"

Andy paused for more large swigs. Then he continued, "Penny hated Scarlett…right from the beginning. She made sure that Scarlett gets the worst and the meanest treatment in the home. She wouldn't leave Scarlett in peace even for a minute. The poor thing had to help with household chores a lot. It was like watching Cinderella all over again, except Scarlett had no escape from there. Sometimes, I tried to stop Penny from being mean but…she was determined to bully Scarlett to the extreme. I couldn't tell Scarlett's father how Penny was treating her, because Scarlett was our best source of income. Her father was sending money while my job wasn't paying well. Besides the good money…Penny was constantly threatening me to remain silent"

"Were you afraid of your wife?"

"Penny was strong. She had always been. She controlled our home. She controlled me and my children.

We were all terrified. I worked for long hours. Penny stayed home. When I returned in the evening, I could only see a glimpse of the torture. It made my heart cry thinking what Scarlett was going through when I was not at home. Penny argued strongly, mentioning that Scarlett had the blood of my sister who had obviously been a proven whore. So, it was likely that Scarlett would end up in a teen pregnancy if she was not disciplined. A couple of years later, to make matters worse for Scarlett, Roy arrived. He was on the loose from some felony and wanted to hide at our place...for a while. During that period, I suspected that he was abusing Scarlett, physically and sexually. I tried asking Scarlett, but she was terrified of Penny...I wanted to contact her father, but she begged me not to mention it to anyone...She was afraid that Roy would kill her. With all my courage, I decided to confront Roy. I asked him to leave the house immediately. He in turn, threatened me that he would expose with my extra marital affair"

Andy paused again, for the beer.

"Wait...", said Tiara, "You had an extra marital affair, but you said you were afraid of you wife"

Andy smiled, "Both are true. At one point, I was tired of my life and was looking for something exciting. It just happened so quickly that I didn't have much time to think about it. One day, while drinking with my mates, I spilled the beans. Roy was drinking with us as well…but…I thought he wasn't sober enough to pay any attention to it. I guess I was wrong. Regardless, I wanted to stop the abuse and told Penny about it. Penny had no interest in saving Scarlett, but she claimed that Scarlett was lying and trying to defame her brother. I tried my best, believe me…but she was too strong. It continued for weeks or perhaps months. I watched the little one …languishing and fading…in front of my eyes. I suppose after a while, Scarlett was numb, and the torture wasn't affecting her anymore. One night, after heavy drinking, I threatened Penny that I'd tell Scarlett's father…everything that she had done to Scarlett so far. Penny wasn't going to lose Scarlett because she was the reason, we were receiving extra money every month. That money was changing our lifestyles. We started buying better clothes, better drinks, and better care for my children. Losing Scarlett would've ended it all. But I think…there was a fallout between Penny and Roy somewhere. The very next day, I saw…Penny kicked Roy out of the home. Roy was in rage. I still remember his red eyes and constant swearing to kill Penny. Like I said, he was a deranged man. He had no mercy on a small child. I'm sure he had no affection for his own sister"

Andy took more swigs. Tiara said mechanically, "You are a coward man Andy. You couldn't protect a child. If you weren't happy with your marriage, you could've broken it long ago but you continued, had an affair and lived in shame. What do you think about all that?"

Andy lowered his head. Perhaps, it was not the first time he thought about it. Reminiscing those days were making him showered in shame naturally. Tiara was wondering how this man lived a normal life all these years. How did he even sleep at night while a child was suffering under the same roof?

Andy continued, "I agree with you kid. I was a coward. I couldn't leave her because I had no money to pay her alimony back then…she wasn't going to leave me without good enough money. Also, I loved my sons a lot. Breaking up at that age was certainly going to affect their lives. But believe me…it still hurts…that I could not save my sister's child. I've never been able to forgive myself for how miserably I failed to provide a safe life to Scarlett"

Jacob had pressed the pause button allowing Andy to soak in his grief for a moment. Tiara focused on scratching her left thumbnail with the right. She had been thinking about wiping out the residual nail color, but the busy recent events were not allowing any time to focus on herself. While Andy was recovering himself, Tiara was able to clean the nail completely. She was not interested in consoling the old man. He was a seasoned loser. And had paid the price for it.

Once Andy was ready again Jacob played the recorder. Tiara asked with the same tone, "The visit to… Cotswold, after many years…what prompted it? What made you suddenly visit the place again?"

"Scarlett planned it"

Tiara gasped, "Scarlett?"

"Yes Scarlett. We hadn't seen her ever since she left us for university. She never phoned or email or sent any messages. She even ignored calls from my sons let alone me or Penny. Apparently…she was happy to cut all ties with us completely. But then, one day, she phoned me on my mobile. Covid was still on, but life was just starting to get normal. We had not visited any place for more than a year already. Scarlett presented the idea of a trip to the same place where we had gone before. She wanted to make the reunion memorable. Penny was completely against it but Scarlett said she was ready to sponsor the trip. It was a breezer for me and I was somehow able to convince Penny. After all, we are Scarlett's only family here"

"Where was Scarlett when the accident happened?"

"Well, she didn't show up"

"What?"

"In the morning after we started driving, she called

me on my mobile to say that she had caught Covid and didn't want to spread it to us. Honestly, we're delighted to have a paid vacation for just the two of us. I remember Penny was ecstatic that she was not going to meet Scarlett"

Tiara was taken aback but she continued, "Anything else you remember about the trip Andy? Anything before the trip? Anyone you met? Any stranger?"

"Nothing that I can recall. Needless to say that... police didn't even ask me this question"

"Did anyone visit your home, any stranger, days or weeks before the trip?"

"Not anyone besides the postman or some local folks. Well, yes, there was someone...a total stranger...a woman. She wanted to sell something to us. I don't remember exactly. Why does it matter whether anyone visited my place? I don't quite understand", Andy asked anxiously.

Tiara cleared her throat and said, "I know you suspect Roy but we're just trying to see if there's a way to prove it. What was the woman trying to sell and how did she look?"

"She...was older than you. Much older. She had brown... or maybe black hair, I don't remember exactly. She came with a proposal of joining some group or a recreation center...or a yoga...I really can't remember.

I'm telling you; Roy killed her. He followed us or sent someone to run over her. Maybe it was himself as you can see Penny walked out at midnight. It couldn't have been a stranger, could it?", Andy tried to resign.

"That's right. I think we've got a lot of information on this case. We are now going to go back and review it. Meanwhile, if you remember anything else you can call us directly. We'll see how we can link it to Roy"

Jacob pressed the stop button.

On the way back home, Jacob was driving the car while Tiara sat with her eyes closed. It was a tiring day. She wanted to get back quickly and start working on her story, perhaps after a glass of lemonade. She opened her eyes and started playing with the music system by changing the radio stations. Jacob said, "Your story now has a string of characters and events. You just need to put them in perspective. I think it's going to sell well"

"You think so?"

"I really do"

"Do you think I should bust this gang?" Tiara asked thoughtfully.

"Uh…I am not sure. You obviously can't mention any real name because that might cause legal implications"

"But how do I stop these people from doing what they are doing?"

"You don't need to stop them. They are going to stop it themselves. Once your story is out, they are going to be nervous thinking that…at least a significant population in the country will know about them. My guess is that these guys will go underground, certainly for a year or even more, if not forever. They'll try to avoid taking any risk. If there are more gangs like them, that too will disappear. These are ordinary people. They're not real criminal gangs. They sure will focus on saving themselves going forward"

"And meanwhile, Scarlett and I will start a new life, somewhere else, over the hills and far away…"

Jacob continued driving for a while without saying a word. Then he uttered, "Are you trying to convince yourself that you're digging this dirt to rescue Scarlet? Does she even know that you are going to publish her story?"

"I mentioned to her about my new job attempt. I did, for sure. But…I…I must have forgotten to tell her the details about it"

Tiara recalled how much she had accused Scarlett of telling lies. A drop of guilt appeared in her mind. Lying to her best friend was not something she was feeling proud of.

20

The next evening, Tiara headed towards Angel. Longer daylights changed the atmosphere around, to a very different one, from the first time she had visited Nadira's home. The cobblestone, the crowded pubs, the noisy Starbucks, plastic glasses rolling on the pathway; were the same as before, but looked dull and uneventful under the daylight, as if someone had scooped the suspense out of the entire scene.

Tiara knew the best time to catch Nadira at home. She was spot on. Nadira opened the door after Tiara rang the doorbell. Tiara, without the Met outfit, was a different person and Nadira didn't fail to notice that. She glanced at Tiara's body and said, "Oh it's you, officer, you alright? Are you off duty today? How can I help you?"

"I am glad you remember me." said Tiara, standing on the first of the three steps of the stairs.

"Of course I do. Is the case still open?"

"Yes it is. I'm still working on it. I'm in different clothes because I was just into a covert operation following someone", Tiara wasn't sure her lies would be convincing, but she had practiced them in front of her bathroom mirror at least five times.

"I see", Nadira closed the door from outside without making any noise and walked down the stairs, "I have some guests inside and my roommate is also in. I wouldn't be comfortable discussing anything crime related in front of them"

"I understand," said Tiara. She noticed that Nadira looked indeed like she was attending guests. Her hair was straightened and shining black. The platinum earrings and little nose pin were there just like last time. Her nails were painted diligently on both fingers and toes. She was glowing all over.

Resting her left leg on the higher stair, Tiara said, "We've almost nailed down a bigger scam behind the entire incident. I'm afraid your late friend Jamal would have to be involved in the investigation as well. We need your help in connecting some missing dots. But…I…am assuring you that you're not going to be involved. Your information will be used but you will be safe. Do you think you want to proceed by helping us?"

Nadia looked anxious and worried. She rubbed

the tip of her nose with the back of her palm. Tiara thought she was beginning to get nervous. Then she said "I think… I would like to bring my lawyer in"

"Well, let me tell you. If you bring your lawyer, then it becomes an official effort from your side. Whatever you then say, will be documented. You might have to get into witness protection and many things like that. It will be a long journey for you and in the process of it, if it so happens that you were part of anything, anything at all, the case against you would go on. So, I was offering you an unofficial account from your knowledge…off the record kind"

Nadira continued thinking, occasionally adjusting her hair and closing eyes. Tiara thought she was perhaps praying. Finally, she said "Alright. What do you want to know?"

"You'll have to work on your memory at this point. I want you to go back to the time when Jamal committed suicide"

"It's painful for me. I hope you understand"

"I do. But we don't have a choice"

"Well then. Ready when you are"

"Do you remember that weekend very well?

"I can't forget that"

"Alright. Do you remember that weekend being the Covid pandemic period?"

"Yes, naturally. What else was there one year ago?"

"And you guys, I mean, you and Jamal were not traveling much?"

"Not at all. Not anywhere"

"Do you know why... Jamal had visited Cotswold on the Saturday before he died and returned on Sunday afternoon?"

Nadira could not answer immediately. After a short pause she said, "He didn't go anywhere. Who told you he went to Cotswold?"

"We have records of his mobile locations. He also had hired a car. Rental people had identified. He drove alone. You were not with him. Can you tell me why?" Tiara had practiced these lines as well in front of her mirror. She was becoming an expert liar.

"He didn't tell me that he had planned the trip. I wasn't involved in wherever he was going or doing. He had told me...he'd have to spend some time with... all those blokes who had shown interest in staging his play. I didn't know anything more than that", Nadira said very quickly. Tiara observed that she was already sweating behind her ears.

"Then why did you just lie to me that he didn't go anywhere?"

"I was frightened. Believe me. I didn't know...

anything more than what I've just said", Nadira said with urgency.

"When did you come to know? Was it right after he came back or a few days later?", Tiara realized she just raised her voice slightly anticipating that it could intimidate Nadira.

"Few days later. When he came back, he didn't speak to me. I thought he was upset. He locked himself in the guest room with his laptop I suppose. I tried to persuade him to come out, but he wasn't listening. He didn't open the door or responded to me. I thought he needed some space. Next day I went to work as usual. When I returned his door was open. He looked completely rattled...as if he just spent years in a prison. We spoke normally about my work, his day which was at home but nothing about his trip. He just didn't say a word. Another day passed by, and I realized that he was not behaving like his usual self. Something...inside...was hurting him. I arranged some good food and drink for us. Normally...he was an earnestly religious Muslim and wouldn't touch alcohol. But that night was different. After four or five drinks, he lost control and started opening up"

"What...did he say?"

Nadira looked down. Hair from the sides dropped to the front covering her face partially. Looking up again pulling the hair to the sides, she said,

"Did he say that he had killed someone?" Tiara asked.

Nadira's eyes were moist. Her lips were shaking,

"He said…he said…that…he was guilty. He was sent in a mission, and he might have been part of a murder"

"Who sent him to mission and who was murdered? Did he say that?"

"He said… yes…I was so scared. I continued asking the same question. He said it was a man named Trent and his friends. The woman named Scarlett was also part of it. He said, they're a gang…they plan to kill people. He was involved in the gang only because…they promised to help him. He had no intention or personal agenda behind the murder. Those people used him… they bullied him get involved in the murder. In fact, he didn't even know the person would be murdered. His task was to bring the woman out of the home at midnight. Trust me, he was not involved in the actual murder"

"Who was murdered?"

"He told me it was an old woman. She was Scarlett's aunt"

"Scarlett got her own aunt murdered. Really?"

"I don't know anything about that…please…I'm just telling you what Jamal had told me. He was guilty and ruined and hurting and everything I can tell you. He was thinking of going to the police and confess the whole thing"

"And what did you tell him?"

"I told him we should go to the police in the morning. Sometimes, confessions can help reduce the sentence. I told him we should put the gang behind the bars"

"Did you?" Tiara looked into the eyes of Nadira sharply. Nadira dropped her eyes.

"Let me tell you what you actually did", Tiara moved one step closer to Nadira, "You consoled him that night because telling him anything in that state of mind would've been useless. The next morning, you told him that, you were going to tell Police that he was involved in the murder unless he listened to what you wanted him to do. Am I saying it right?"

Nadira's eyes broke into tears, her nostrils flared, knees folded. She sat down on the stairs while weeping. Then she said, "I didn't want to lose this opportunity. He was a weak man already and became even weaker with that incident. It was my golden chance to control his life...he told me once that Scarlett always had readily available money with her. I wasn't not doing very well at work then. What you see me now is very different from those days. I needed some money...so I ordered him to start blackmailing Scarlett about the murder. That was going to get me a good amount of money...I could control Jamal, and…also have constant inflow of money…he would be under complete mercy of my mood…If I said jump and he wouldn't ask where"

"Is that how you planned to treat your lover?"

Nadira continued weeping, "I feel so terrible about everything…I can't tell you how much regret it is. Looking back, I don't know what I was thinking. As if I was possessed, by a spirit"

"So what happened after that?"

"I went to work as normal but was keeping a tab on him. We spoke over the phone a few times during the day, and he said that he was working on his plan to talk to Scarlett. When I returned from work, he was already dead. My world had suddenly hit the ground reality…I had lost Jamal…I can never forget that moment when I saw him dead. Rest of it was in police records. No one suspected me. It was a clean case of suicide. He even left a note that… due to his chronic failure in establishing himself he was ending his life", Nadira continued weeping. Tiara stood by the stairs with her hands on the hips.

Night dropped in like a thick blanket. Lights were turned on all around the houses. Faint noises started appearing behind Nadira's closed doors. Tiara wondered whether the guests were still waiting for Nadira's return.

Nadira looked up, wiped her eyes, sniffled big and said, "Do you think…I am going to prison for this?"

"I'm not going to make a case against you. I'm trying to catch the real murderer, not you. In fact, there is no case against you. Unless you told me, no one would ever be able to prove what you had done"

Nadira continued looking at Tiara as if she couldn't comprehend Tiara's words. Then she said, "But I'm a terrible person. Am I not? Don't I deserve any punishment?"

Tiara started getting down the stairs, it was time she moved on, "You were the reason your lover died. Then you had many months…to mourn…before I showed up. I don't know how…on earth… you passed those months alone. I'd certainly like to know one day. I imagine it was very hard. Were you sleeping at night? Were you afraid of being caught? Only you can tell…If you think that wasn't enough of a punishment, think again. You know what you actually did? You bullied him to death. He was fighting against bullies but how could he know that there was one right under his roof?"

Tiara turned back and started walking away. Nadira sat behind, motionless, as if the ground beneath her feet would fall apart when she moved.

21

Every day, around six in the evening, Trent would get out of his office building, walk towards the tube station two blocks away, ride the tube for about thirty minutes, arrive at his station in Brixton and walk to his home that was five minutes away. Tiara was able to follow Trent without any trouble for two consecutive days; just to make sure his routine was always the same, every day. Plugged in with his iPhone EarPods and reading a book inside the train, Trent never looked around; even though Tiara stood in the same compartment, wearing a black covid mask, almost unrecognizable in the evening crowd. Trent had no interest in the world around. He was a busy man.

On the third day, Tiara waited outside his home for exactly ten minutes after he went inside. Then she knocked on the door. Trent lived in a small house inside a community. The cheek by jowl houses packed inside the gated area, looked all the same; made of brick red color, gray windows, a chimney pointing up at the top and a black horseshoe at the front door. There was a large brown doormat in front of Trent's door with the word 'Welcome' printed on it. Although unnecessary, Tiara rubbed her shoe on the mat. It felt amusing.

A woman of around Trent's age, opened the door. Tiara thought she must be Trent's wife. She wore a blue skirt and matching blue blouse with high collars. Her face was round, and lips were large.

Tiara quickly introduced herself and explained that she had some work with Trent. The woman brought her inside and offered to sit on a bar stool by the kitchen counter. There were two stools, made of black leather, in front of the counter. Tiara realized that she had been visiting many homes since she got involved in this matter. This time, the room was much better organized and meticulously decorated. The woman meant cleanliness; there was no sign of any dirt anywhere in the room. There was a costly rug with old war painting like designs on it; there were Chinese flower vases standing on the ground, reclining sofas and glass shelves. There was a painting on the wall displaying a lily flower which Tiara could recognize as impressionist painting. She had learned that at school. There was a famous French painter who painted lilies whole life, but Tiara could not remember his name.

The woman opened a cupboard in the kitchen, placed two cookies out of a jar on a pretty white porcelain saucer and handed it to Tiara. After Tiara gratefully accepted the snack, the woman asked courteously, "Would you like some tea?" As Tiara politely refused, the woman excused herself to look for Trent inside. Tiara thought he must have been taking a shower.

Within five minutes Trent appeared. He indeed was in shower as Tiara noticed his hair looked partially wet, he wore a white shirt, and his razor thin glass frames were shining under the light.

"Tiara...what a pleasant surprise", He was genuinely surprised. Tiara noticed that he missed buttoning the top part of his shirt in the rush to come out.

"I was just passing by and thought of surprising you", Tiara knew that Trent wouldn't believe it.

Trent stood at the other side of the counter. Before he said anything his wife appeared from the bedroom and asked, "Would you like a cup of tea?"

"No, I'm fine. Please go inside", Trent raised his right hand without looking at her.

"You must be hungry. It was a long day..." Before she could complete the sentence Trent stepped near her, wrapped his arm around her waist and kissed her.

Without waiting for her reaction Trent said, "I'm in a very busy meeting. Please don't disturb us"

The woman turned back quietly and walked inside.

"What on earth are you doing here?", Trent whispered. He was visibly disturbed.

"Let me get straight to the point", Tiara adjusted herself on the stool, "I'm here for your confession?"

"My what?", Trent still maintained the low tone.

"Your confession"

"What confession?"

"You know it. You were involved in the murder of Mrs. Penelope Baker, almost a year ago. You ran a vehicle over her."

"What rubbish? What are you talking about?", Trent looked still disturbed and cautious.

"She was Scarlett's aunt and also…was Scarlett's bully, in your terms. Both of you planned to murder her. Helen and Jamal were also involved. Scarlett organized a trip for them in Cotswold, Jamal followed them there. At night Jamal was able to lure the woman out of her cottage when you ran over her. All this is fact", Tiara narrated with a straight face.

"This is bollocks. Scarlett's aunt died in an accident. I was not involved by any means. We had a different plan for her", Trent turned around towards the bedroom cautiously while uttering the words carefully.

"Is that so? Let me tell you that Scarlett has already confessed. She is ready to go to prison but only along with you", Tiara realized she was now able to twist facts conveniently according to her choice. She also realized that she no longer needed the protection of concentric circles while talking to anyone.

"Scarlett said that! Oh my god...", Trent cringed his face and placed his right palm into his hairline. His body bent over the counter to support from falling.

"She did", Tiara continued, "And now it's your turn to accept the fact"

"And what's your role here? Are you a cop now? Are you wired? Is someone listening at the other end?"

"I'm neither a cop nor I'm wired. I'm just here to provide you a choice"

"I don't have a choice if Scarlett is betraying the oath. We were supposed to be all for one. We have been helping each other feel better over the years. You know everything about that.... Scarlett's aunt's turn arrived, and we planned it together. Our intention was to injure her...so badly that...she could only crawl for the rest of her life but...it went all wrong...terribly wrong... the accident killed her on the spot. It was an accident... believe me. We didn't have any intention to kill her"

"How convenient. Why does it happen time and

again? You guys, try to hurt someone and then call it an accident? Isn't it too convenient?"

Trent's wife appeared again from the door and started to walk towards the kitchen. Trent sprang back on her feet quickly, wrapped his arms around her and walked her back to her room as if he was taking his child for a walk.

"You love your wife a lot"

"That's none of your business. We are talking about the accident and that is all. Yes, the accident; do you know why it happens? Because we are ordinary people. We are not trained criminals. We just wanted to change the world to a better place. We are not bad people at all"

"Who decides good or bad Trent? There's only a thin line between the two. One moment you are a good man, the very next moment you cross the line, and you are bad"

"Look at my plight", Trent scoffed, "A generation Z is teaching me what's good and what's bad. What do you guys know about life? Your generation has spent ninety percent of their lives by sticking their noses in a smartphone. What have you learnt about the world yet?"

"Do you want to know what I've learnt? I now know…how to identify people like you who can't see what their true self is. Look at you. You have no idea what you've become while hunting bullies. You are no less than a bully. You keep hurting people in the name of revenge. How about they hurt you back again? What will you call it? Accident? Or you hurt them back and start a war?"

Trent removed his glasses to rub his eyes. He was thinking, deep.

Tiara continued, "You guys have caused enough damage to many people. It's time you stop it"

"What are you going to do? Hand me over to the cops"

"No. I just want you to disappear. You know what disappearing means? You leave this home, this city, your current job, social media, everything you have currently…both online and in real life. No one will ever…ever know where you are and what you are doing. If you leave the group, it's going to break. You are the heart of it"

"And Scarlett?"

"She will disappear too. Maybe in a different country"

Trent stayed silent for a moment. He strolled in the small kitchen from one end to the other, rubbing his both hands together; then he said, "What if I don't agree with you. Do you really think even Scarlett can prove that I killed her aunt? The case is going to run for a very long time"

Tiara stepped down from the stool. It was not much of a comfort sitting on it anymore. She picked up her handbag and said in her most serious tone "I'll expose you. I have powerful contacts in news agencies. They're going to publish everything you guys have been doing. And you…will be the villain of the story. Remember, it's not the hand that holds the sword, but the hand that holds the pen, writes history"

Trent was not blinking. He perhaps was regretting why Tiara was included in their plan.

Tiara continued, "Besides, your loving wife and your family must know the reality about you. They are going to know how you're running after people with revenge in mind"

"They are not going to believe you"

"They sure will. There'll be a whole bunch of evidence against you. And there will be Scarlett, who was your lover once upon a time"

"What?"

"You cheated on your wife with Scarlett. Didn't you?"

Trent was unable to speak. Tiara continued "When you met Scarlett you were already married and had children. You were on the dating app. How will you explain that? I'm sure it wasn't only Scarlett. You were involved with many other women. Your wife is going to learn all that…"

"Are you going to blackmail me?"

"I'm just crossing the line from good to bad. You may ask why I chose to do so. Because I'm trying to stop this bloodshed...been a long time...let's all go home. Hunting is over"

THE LAST CHAPTER

Urban Legends are created out of ordinary lives. They are often born in ordinary neighborhoods on small lanes or alleys or pavements. They then flow around, in whispers, in songs, poetries, bedtime stories, websites, blogs, videos and memes. They become viral. Tiara's report on bully hunting was destined to become an urban legend.

After many reviews and edits by Jacob, it was finally published in both the online and printed editions. Initial feedback from the board was extremely encouraging and to her delight, she was offered the job. Jacob then turned the offer into a more lucrative one to suit exactly what Tiara needed. It was a position in Chicago. Besides the preparation for the move to America and its immigration, she had many hurdles to cross, in terms of going through some training on the depths of journalism, but she was floating at the cloud nine already.

Then one summer morning, when the bright sun was about to cruise its way up, Tiara, after making the right turn from the alley, would make her way through her usual running pathway; meeting the known faces like she had been doing every day. This time some of them would stop to congratulate her for writing the wonderful piece of news article. They would say encouraging words about Tiara's talent and glowing future. The same would follow over email and Instagram accounts. She would spend hours every day responding to several different types of questions and comments. She would start tweeting as well where people write about their experiences on bullying and its consequences. Her followers would discuss her article, the story of bully hunting and even Omni, which would now fall under Tiara's umbrella. Tiara would post about practicing compassion and forgiveness and receive millions of comments. Out of nowhere, she would turn into an online influencer with thousands of followers. With a large smile on her face, she would look into her bathroom mirror. The old glass with lots of water marks on it, would remain trustworthy to show her the same reflection as every single day; but this time, Tiara would look at herself carefully. She would notice a woman emerging with confidence. The woman was an achiever, someone, almost famous. For a moment, she would try to focus on the eyes of the reflection. Behind the dark shades of liners, she would only see eyes of deceit and betrayal. She was successful in turning the tide to her benefit, at the expense of Trent and others, including Scarlett.

On another summer afternoon, when a breeze carrying small dust particles blew over the concrete streets, Tiara would take the train to Brixton, walk five minutes from the station and arrive at the house with black horseshoe and the brown doormat with Welcome sign. The house would remain locked, and no one would open the door after many knocks. Just to be certain, Tiara would ask a neighbor and the neighbor would confirm that Trent and family had indeed disappeared. Another day, she would phone Boris who was preparing for a move to his new property by the sea in Portugal. His voice would sound content and relaxed, congratulating Tiara for everything she had achieved. On another dry afternoon, her stop would be Stella's door where she would learn that Stella's parents were soon going to arrive. Meanwhile, Barbara, elated about all recent movements, would spend hundreds of pounds shopping for Tiara's clothes, to beat the notorious winds of Chicago. Barbara would cook all favorite dishes for Tiara, and they would spend late nights watching movies together. Barbara would also announce her vacation with friends from the nursing community to Dubrovnik. Life had never been so kind to her.

As for Scarlett, she would look forward to her move to upstate New York where she had been admitted for masters, starting from the coming Fall. Her father would be just a few hours' drive away and Tiara would be a couple of hours flight away. She would be waiting to leave her earlier life behind to start another from scratch. Days before leaving her apartment for good, she would stand in front of the window with Tiara beside her. They would discuss the events that were taking place on the very first day and giggle about everything. The gorgeous night lights of the decorated city would stare at them with encouragement. High above, a full moon would try to mingle with the lights at the tallest building. A clear spotless sky, under the glowing orange moon, would appear to be converging with the land, with city lights far away shining like tiny twinkles. Tiara would look from the east to the west as far as her vision could reach. From the far east, Stella's home to the far west where Scarlett's family lived long ago. From way up north, her neighborhood and to the south where Trent lived. Those imaginary dots were connected by a labyrinth of endless streets where bullies operated every day and every night. Often, some of them were punished by a group of people who called themselves hunters. They were carefully hidden underground, until the day Tiara met Scarlett in her first investigation. Gratefully turning to Scarlett, Tiara would kiss her lips, gently. Scarlett's body would respond with a soft tremor. Moments later, from the tiny twinkles to the magnificent moon, every object that emitted light that night, would turn their eyes away, for the two bodies to melt together in harmony.

Urban Legends operate in their own manner. Over a period of time, they mold in many directions, changing the characters to much larger than they actually were. A very successful person once said that it's not important who you are but what matters is which story you are a part of. Scarlett was part of the legend from its origin. She also deserved to be the owner of it, but Tiara was quick to steal the glory from her. Tiara could never successfully confess her guilt near her, as she would place her index finger at Tiara's lips, whenever Tiara started the conversation. Scarlett, perhaps never wanted to talk about it anymore. Perhaps, she was hurt. After reaching Chicago, Tiara had received just a message from Scarlett that she too had reached safely. Ever since that day, Scarlett had removed all means of communications with Tiara. She never shared her phone number, removed all social media accounts and never responded to email. Scarlett's father too was not reachable. After numerous attempts, Tiara concluded that Scarlett wanted to disappear from her past. Tiara just knew too much about her. It was no surprise that Scarlett was not feeling safe near someone who had access to her dark secrets and a large presence in social media at the same time. Tiara remembered the night, when standing at the Embankment, Scarlett told her how she could create awareness about bullying, ripples all over social media and more. Tiara had overtaken her to throw the pebble in the pond first. Scarlett was wounded by the betrayal.

Almost a decade later, Tiara is a busy woman traveling to different parts of the world. She could be seen on a picturesque hiking trail in Bogota or sipping latte macchiato, at a sea facing tiny cafe in sultry Bari or cycling on the busy streets of sunny Brisbane. A famous online persona and a freelance journalist, Tiara is successful and motivated. In her busy life, she has made hundreds of new friends, met thousands of new people, both on and offline. Jacob continues to be in constant touch through work. There's no other friend from her past life anymore. She still misses Scarlett occasionally. At her leisure hours, when Tiara is not working on anything, her mind no longer brings pictures of her old childhood days with Stella, but it ignites the memories of those few months with Scarlett. Looking back, she wonders how real Scarlett actually was. Sometimes, Tiara wonders whether Scarlett even existed or was just an imaginary imposition of her alter ego on someone else. She can't remember every detail of her interaction, but she finds it strange how some of Scarlett's attributes and life structure were exactly opposite of Tiara's. She gets goosebumps thinking that she might have been talking to her alter ego during those days. Was she hallucinating? But from deep inside, Tiara knows that the real Scarlett must be out there somewhere, perhaps on the most common locations; like on Tiara's hiking trails or in the cafes or the bike lanes. A Scarlett, emerges from ordinary people and lives an ordinary life until she becomes a legend. Whenever Tiara comes across a young ginger woman with red frame glasses, her heart stops for a moment with anticipation. She tries to talk to the woman only to realize quickly that she was probably looking for slightly shorter hair or narrower eyes or longer nose. Her search for the real Scarlett continues and she believes that Scarlett will certainly appear, on a new day, in a new story.

The End

Printed in the United States
by Baker & Taylor Publisher Services